Slash

Also From Laurelin Paige

Man in Charge Duet
Man in Charge
Man in Love

Slay Series
Slay One: Rivalry
Slay Two: Ruin
Slay Three: Revenge
Slay Four: Rising
Slash: A Slay Novella

The Fixed Series
Fixed on You
Found in You
Forever with You
Hudson
Falling Under You: A Fixed Trilogy Novella (1001 Dark Nights)
Chandler
Dirty, Filthy Fix: A Fixed Trilogy Novella (1001 Dark Nights)
Fixed Forever

Dirty Universe
Dirty Filthy Rich Boys
Dirty Filthy Rich Men
Dirty Filthy Rich Love
Dirty, Sexy Player
Dirty Sexy Games
Sweet Liar
Sweet Fate
Dirty Sweet Valentine
Wild Rebel

Found Duet
Free Me
Find Me

Slash

A Slay Series Novella

By Laurelin Paige

1001 DARK NIGHTS
PRESS

Slash
A Slay Series Novella
By Laurelin Paige

1001 Dark Nights
Copyright 2020 Laurelin Paige
ISBN: 978-1-951812-13-3

Foreword: Copyright 2014 M. J. Rose

Cover photo credit © Annie Ray/ Passion Pages

Published by 1001 Dark Nights Press, an imprint of Evil Eye Concepts, Incorporated

Acknowledgments from the Author

To my family—Thank you for the best albums of memories. I'm lucky to have shelves and shelves stacked with your love.

To Liz Berry, Jillian Stein, and MJ Rose—I'm inspired by you and so honored to be in your family. And to you, Liz, especially for trusting my telling of this story. It was what I needed to write, and you let it grow into what it needed to be.

To my tribe: Rebecca Friedman, Candi Kane, Melissa Gaston, Roxie Madar, Kayti McGee, Melanie Harlow, Lauren Blakely, C.D. Reiss, Amy "Vox" Libris – You've made a crazy, terrible time feel so much more bearable. I wouldn't survive a pandemicalypse without you.

To my readers—Thank you for letting me explore this ugly, broken, beautiful world with you. I'm eternally grateful you've come along for this ride.

To my God—Help me to remember to always wonder and love. Thank you for being patient all the times that I've forgotten.

Sign up for the 1001 Dark Nights Newsletter
and be entered to win a Tiffany Key necklace.

There's a contest every month!

Go to www.1001DarkNights.com to subscribe.

**As a bonus, all subscribers can download
FIVE FREE exclusive books!**

One Thousand and One Dark Nights

Once upon a time, in the future…

*I was a student fascinated with stories and learning.
I studied philosophy, poetry, history, the occult, and
the art and science of love and magic. I had a vast
library at my father's home and collected thousands
of volumes of fantastic tales.*

*I learned all about ancient races and bygone
times. About myths and legends and dreams of all
people through the millennium. And the more I read
the stronger my imagination grew until I discovered
that I was able to travel into the stories... to actually
become part of them.*

*I wish I could say that I listened to my teacher
and respected my gift, as I ought to have. If I had, I
would not be telling you this tale now.
But I was foolhardy and confused, showing off
with bravery.*

*One afternoon, curious about the myth of the
Arabian Nights, I traveled back to ancient Persia to
see for myself if it was true that every day Shahryar
(Persian: شهريار, "king") married a new virgin, and then
sent yesterday's wife to be beheaded. It was written
and I had read that by the time he met Scheherazade,
the vizier's daughter, he'd killed one thousand
women.*

*Something went wrong with my efforts. I arrived
in the midst of the story and somehow exchanged
places with Scheherazade – a phenomena that had
never occurred before and that still to this day, I
cannot explain.*

*Now I am trapped in that ancient past. I have
taken on Scheherazade's life and the only way I can
protect myself and stay alive is to do what she did to
protect herself and stay alive.*

*Every night the King calls for me and listens as I spin tales.
And when the evening ends and dawn breaks, I stop at a
point that leaves him breathless and yearning for more.
And so the King spares my life for one more day, so that
he might hear the rest of my dark tale.*

*As soon as I finish a story... I begin a new
one... like the one that you, dear reader, have before
you now.*

Introduction

Foreground: The area of an image—usually a photograph, drawing, or painting—that appears closest to the viewer. - *MoMA Glossary of Art Terms*

There's no way to see an entire life in a single photograph. It takes a portfolio, an expansive collection to understand the nuances of character and experience and circumstance.

Still, there can be a complete story in a snapshot. A good photographer knows how to find that narrative, knows which moments are worth capturing and which aren't. A good photographer can adjust the lens just right, so the background becomes hazy and unimportant and undistracting. A good photographer knows when the foreground is enough to tell the story that needs to be told. A good photographer focuses in and snaps at just the right time.

That's what the snobbiest of professional photographers say—that the perfect shots are planned and executed with precision. I've said it myself on several occasions, when my work has been acclaimed, when I'm feeling prideful about my compositions.

If I'm being honest, I don't know that there's much reason to boast about any of the photos that have earned me attention. Most of the time, I just got lucky.

Chapter One

Cropping: Editing, typically by removing the outer edges of the image. -
MoMA Glossary of Art Terms

You've got to be kidding me.

The thought races through my mind repeatedly as I shuffle through the registration papers in front of me, as if I might have the wrong stack, as if I might see something different when I return to the sheet with the names of all my students.

Of course nothing changes when my eyes return to the enrollment form. There are still thirteen names arranged in alphabetical order. There are still more women than men by a three to one ratio. And Hendrix Reid is still the last male name on the list.

It can't be a coincidence. It's bloody unlikely there are many Hendrixes in the photography world, less unlikely more than one of them has the surname Reid.

Despite the unlikelihood, I hold on to the slim thread of doubt, mainly because I have no other choice. I have no time to prepare mentally for the alternative since class is set to begin in, oh, four and a half minutes. A good majority of the thirteen students are already sitting at the three tables squaring the room in front of me, and since none of them are recognizable, it isn't impossible that the Hendrix Reid enrolled is not *my* Hendrix Reid.

Not that I have a Hendrix Reid. He was never actually mine. Even for the one night we spent together, we remained strangers. Sure, we took our clothing off and engaged in wicked behavior, but the lights were out so it was more anonymous than not, despite having exchanged names, which I try to never do. Technically, I hadn't then either. The conference we'd attended had taken care of that, listing both our names and our bios with headshots in the event directory, without any regard to the fact that some of us became photographers because we preferred to remain on the other side of the lens.

Which is neither here nor there.

I would have told him my name anyway and with no regrets. The conversation that had led to the tryst in his hotel room had been rather remarkable, and a lot of it had centered around the fact that we were both notable photographers, so anonymity wasn't ever going to apply between us.

And why would famed wildlife photographer Hendrix Reid be registered for a portrait course, in London, of all places? He'd told me he was wintering in the savannahs, and while spring is definitely upon us now, there is not much in the way of wildlife here beyond the hedgehogs and kestrels at Regent's Park. Certainly nothing to attract him. The idea it's the same man is ludicrous.

Except, hadn't he said he was sure that we would see each other again one day?

I bite the inside of my lip so that I won't audibly groan.

I was stupid not to go through the enrollment form earlier. Strike that, I was cowardly. I'd been nervous about the prospect of teaching the class in the first place. Almost immediately after agreeing to lead the advanced course, I'd wanted to back out. It had been my brother who had convinced me it was a good idea, for reasons I can no longer remember, and why am I listening to his advice about how I live my life these days when he's practically settled in New York with his new wife and child? It's not like he knows what I need now any more than any of the other times we've been apart over the course of our lives, and he's halfheartedly tried to parent me from afar.

I listened to him, though, because while I am well into adulthood and a single mother/career woman who doesn't need governing, I also sort of do.

"Do you actually live your life?" he'd asked, and how dare he, but also maybe thank goodness he dared because I didn't have a good answer to the question, and though I very much objected to his right to know, it was probably something my therapist would want me to consider. Just. There was a reason I didn't see her anymore, and it wasn't because I'd achieved mental clarity.

Rather, like in all things that scared me, I was the type to lower my head, as I had with Hendrix. As I had with this class.

One and a half minutes to go.

One minute.

I watch the seconds tick by on the analog clock hanging on the wall, one of those old-fashioned kinds that dictated time in every class I'd attended through secondary school.

Forty-five seconds.

Thirty seconds and there are now twelve students bowed down over their mobiles. None of them are Hendrix, and my confidence bolsters. He chickened out. He registered as a joke. He registered by accident. Whatever the reason, he's not here, and I'm calmer by the second.

And then the big hand is on the twelve, the little hand perfectly pointed to the ten, and it's time to begin this ludicrous teaching experiment.

With a deep breath, I gather my stack of papers and approach the podium. "Good morning, fellow photographers. As you likely already know, I'm Camilla Fasbender, art director of Accelecom Media, which is a rather fancy title to say I get final approval of the company's branding materials while other more talented artists do all the work and get none of the credit so thank goodness this course isn't meant to instruct in that arena because, really, I know nothing."

The students chuckle—is that an appropriate word for adult learners? It seems so odd when at least three of the faces I'm looking at appear older than me, reminding me how unqualified I feel to be standing before them.

Which is silly. Because I am qualified. *"Find the proof,"* Dr. Joseph used to say, and the proof is that, while it isn't my day job, my portrait photography is revered in some circles, and I do have things that I can share. A whole lesson plan, in fact. I'd managed to pull my head out of the sand long enough to put one together, fortunately, and it wasn't as hard as it might have been because I do know what I'm talking about.

But just as I'm about to confidently plummet on, the door swings open and a tall, muscular figure slinks in, taking the last available chair and sending my heart up to my throat even before his eyes meet mine, and I'm locked in the gaze of Hendrix Reid. *My* Hendrix Reid.

Bloody hell.

That four and a half minutes did nothing to prepare me. Even if I'd spent it actually believing I might come face-to-face with my one-night stand, I still would have been breathless from the shock of seeing him. His sun-tanned face and light brown eyes are quite breathtaking all on their own. Add to that his broad shoulders and sculpted jaw and a muscular frame that somehow moves lithely despite its bulk, and seriously, how can anyone be expected to bother with oxygen when looking in his direction? He's the kind of man who is beautiful enough to model and yet too spectacular to photograph. The light hits him too evenly. There aren't nearly enough shadows to tell a story that isn't about how perfect he is to look at, and stories about perfection become boring really fast so I avoid using my lens to tell them like the plague.

I can't imagine ever getting bored gazing at that face without a lens between us, though. His perfection is captivating in a way that can't be captured. There's something about his features that reflect what they see, but it's only interesting in real life, when the elements around him are present. He doesn't work cropped down to just him. He's meant to be seen in context.

I, on the other hand, prefer to not be seen at all.

Which is why I'm mortified that he's here. It would be one thing if there were a one-way glass between us, where I could look and look until I'd had my fill—if I'd ever have my fill. It's quite another when he's here with nothing between us but this podium, and my looking is met with his looking back.

Obviously, I lose my train of thought.

I have notes, but all the words seem to blur together, and I can't make meaning out of any of the pen strokes. My pulse takes off like it's a locomotive without a destination, my hands are clammy, and thirteen pairs of eyes are staring at me, waiting for me to say something worthwhile. Imagining them all naked is not helpful when I actually know what one of them looks like in the buff.

Well, my hands know, anyway. I did mention the lights had been off.

"Enough about me," I say, as though I've said anything about me at all. "I want to hear about you. What made you decide to enroll? What do you hope to learn? Let's start over here, shall we?" I look at the chair farthest from Hendrix and his perfect everything. "Tell us about yourself."

"Kaila Morrison" seems glad to take the baton. She gives us all a spiel about her photographic aspirations and her career ambitions as well as providing us with a not-so-brief resume. It is an advanced course, after all.

No one was allowed to enroll without submitting a portfolio, all screened by the London Academy of Art, thankfully, or not so thankfully since I would have been able to avoid the Hendrix disaster had I been involved with curating submissions.

What would I have done if I'd come across his registration form? Would I have tossed it out immediately or reached out to him or...what? I dwell on that when I should be more attentive to Kaila.

Then, instead of listening to the next student as he speaks, I berate myself for my preoccupation which doesn't get any better by the time the third student is introducing herself.

Needless to say, by the time we've reached Hendrix, I've learned very little about the people I'm meant to be teaching, and, worse, I'm no better prepared to actually teach them.

When he speaks, though, I'm completely present. Time slows down and the room is suddenly quieter as it disappears into background, and all there is to capture my focus is him.

"I thought it was time to widen my scope of the art," he says, and it feels like he's talking only to me. "I know how to capture an animal as it moves stealthily in its habitat. I know how to adjust my camera for all versions of natural light. I don't have a single clue where to begin when it comes to photographing a person in a studio."

I haven't commented on anyone's introduction thus far, and yet I'm compelled to pry now. "And you've suddenly been met with an abundance of requests to shoot portraits? Don't tell me National Geographic isn't giving you work anymore."

"Uh, no," he laughs. "National Geographic and I are fine." His smile fades from his lips, but it lingers in his eyes. "There's more to life than just the job, though. This whole life of mine began for me with snapping pictures of things I liked to look at. Then it became something else, and I love it. I do. But it's been a long time since there's been any passion."

"And you think that you'll find that here?" My tone verges on hostile, but it is what it is. The words are already out, and there's nothing I can do to flower the message after the fact.

"Yes," he says, and my next breath comes easier for some unknown reason. "Yes, I think I will."

I go through the rest of the class in a daze. I manage to stick to my talking points, for the most part, besides the random time I sidetrack to recommend Nightsky, my favorite bar that happens to be in the vicinity of the Academy campus with decent priced top-shelf drinks and live music and an ambiance that draws me in no matter how terrible the cover bands are. How I got talking about London nightlife is beyond me except that I'm sure it has to do with Hendrix and memories of that dive of a bar that we ended up in that evening last September in France, both of us content because of the company despite the dreadful service.

Somehow I find my way back to the planned topic after that meandering, and somehow I manage to teach something, though I'm only sure that I make sense because of the nods of understanding coming from my pupils. Twelve of them, anyway. Twelve rapt students who give me their full attention, which I'm certain I don't deserve.

I can't bring myself to give Hendrix any attention. It's easier to stumble on, pretending that he's not in the picture.

Ignoring him physically doesn't work to draw my mind from him, however. As I lecture about the basics of portraiture and the art of creating concepts, I'm thinking about him and why he's here and what he said and what it could mean. We did have a passionate night together. Not just in the bedroom, but definitely in the bedroom, where he made me feel for one glorious encounter like my body wasn't a hindrance or a prison for my soul but instead that it was *part* of my soul. There, in the dark, with his mouth at my ear and his hands on my skin, he made *me* feel like the story that needed to be told.

But it was a one-night stand. Silly to think of it as anything more. Even if I were someone who was in the market for something real or long-lasting, it would be ridiculous to hedge any bets after just one encounter.

Hendrix didn't strike me as ridiculous. Or impulsive. Or silly.

Why on earth, then, would he believe that there could be something worth seeking out with me? If that's what he meant at all. Which...he did, didn't he?

It's confusing, and confusion makes me hide, on the whole. But since I can't hide because I'm the fucking teacher in this class—seriously, how did this happen?—and for some reason the educator is expected to stay present, I find my confusion turning to anger. It works itself through me until the beauty of our night together is cropped out of my memory and what's left is trite and fleeting. His presence feels nothing like flattery—which it did feel flattering, admittedly, for a half second there in the midst of everything else. Now, though, it just feels invasive and unprofessional and mean.

Perhaps I'd confront him about it, if I were a different sort of person, one who isn't afraid to stand up to a challenge. One who isn't afraid to live her life.

But I'm not that sort of person, so after I give out the assignments and send the students on their way, I plan to gather my things and get on my way as soon as possible, so fond of hiding that I am. I was stupid enough to believe—or perhaps hopeful is the better term—that Hendrix would let me do that, as he'd let me leave that night in Paris, not that I'd given him a choice.

He doesn't, though, of course. *Of course.* He approaches me, his leather camera bag slung over his shoulder, a man satchel underneath.

"Camilla," he says in that American accent that makes me both cringe and swoon all at once, and for the briefest of moments I find myself considering something different for a change. I consider staying.

But underneath my long sleeve polo neck, my skin throbs with an intensity that equals the blaring of a car alarm, and I think of Fred waiting for me at home to take him out for ice cream and the dead husband who hurt me as much as he loved me and the ugliness that marks me inside and out. And in the chaos of those thoughts, there is no option to stay.

"You being here is in bad taste," I say before he has a chance to say anything else. "Don't do this to me."

I brush past him then, and with the heat of that brief contact following me in radiating waves, I rush outside to disappear among the Saturday-morning Londoners who are out enjoying the early signs of spring.

Chapter Two

Color: The perceived hue of an object, produced by the manner in which it reflects or emits light into the eye. - *MoMA Glossary of Art Terms*

I stare at my empty glass, wondering if I should order a second negroni. Wondering if that will be enough to douse the thoughts of Hendrix. I refuse to look at them, but he's there at the edges of my mind, stirring like the late embers of a fire, or perhaps they're early embers.

I don't want them to be. God help me if this is just the beginning of this spiral.

It's cause to consider that second drink.

But when the bartender passes by, I don't flag him. Not yet. I will, eventually, because I always do. A trip to the bar is never just a one-drink sort of experience. I suppose that some might say I'm an alcoholic, and maybe I am, though I don't tend to crave booze in any form, and I can easily go weeks without a drop.

I have other vices that are much more tempting.

And when those temptations become more vivid, when they transform into foes that have me in a wrestling match, pinned to the mat and about to give in, that's when I find myself sitting in front of some sort of cocktail. It's not the healthiest distraction, but it tends to work. And when it doesn't, sex is another useful diversion.

I hate to think of what impression I might give to a stranger who spent a significant amount of time observing these habits of mine. What would be said of me? What conclusions would be drawn? Does my behavior tonight color the rest of my actions? Would I be slapped with one of those derogatory labels that tend to say as much about the person labeling as the one being labeled?

Lush.

Slut.

Poor excuse for a mother.

No, I won't entertain that last one. I'm a good mother. I'd give my life for my son. If Frank hadn't died, I would have left him for Freddie's sake. No questions asked. I never would have considered leaving before getting pregnant. Back then, I took what I was given. I didn't even run, and hiding always did more harm than good.

That was more than six years ago, that little voice says in the back of my head. It's a nasty nag of a voice, one that tends to love to bully and belittle and is especially loud on the days that I find myself sitting in a crowded bar.

I know how to speak to her, though. *Where's the proof?*

I fiddle with the orange peel dressing the edge of my glass as I count the motherly actions I've performed in the past week. I worked. I earned an income. I got out of bed.

That last one is sometimes frighteningly the hardest.

And though I've left him with the weekend nanny, who arrives at nine AM Saturday morning and doesn't leave until nine AM the next day, I always, always, always spend all of Sunday with him. I deserve this one night to myself. How I use this time bears no reflection on the kind of mother I am. Bears no reflection on the kind of human I am.

Say it enough times, maybe I'll believe it.

The volume of the environment drops significantly as the band quits for a break. The quiet amplifies the noise in my head, but also makes me more aware of my surroundings. I feel the figure sidle up beside me before I see him, and when I look, it's only a quick glance out my periphery, noting the strong forearm protruding from a rolled-up sleeve leaning on the bar at my side.

"Negroni, stirred, on the rocks," he says, and then I have to look more closely, even though I already recognize him. If his thick American accent hadn't given him away, the order surely would have.

I forget to breathe before I lift my eyes, which is a mistake, because as always, the wind is knocked out of me at the sight of him. He's dressed himself up since class this morning. The same jeans maybe—hard to tell without standing back and fully ogling him—but now he's exchanged his

T-shirt for a crisp white dress shirt and a waistcoat that shows off his trim build. His face had been smoothly shaved earlier. Now stubble peppers his jaw and I'm slammed with a haptic memory of the burn of his rough jaw against the sensitive skin of my inner thighs.

I blink the thought away and raise my eyes to his.

"Make that two," he says to the bartender, his gaze locked with mine.

I like being the focal point of his gaze. Whatever he sees when looking at me reflects back, and it's like he's turned on a light in this dark section of the bar. It's like that light is me.

But I didn't come here to be light. I didn't come here to be seen.

Once again, rage courses through my veins. He's already infiltrated my professional life, registering for my class like he did. Now he's trying to steal my recreational life as well?

He can't have it. He can't have any more of me than he already has. I won't let him.

It's only the intensity of my need to protect this one sacred space that gives me the energy for an outburst. "No," I say clearly. Firmly.

Not helpful, really, since I've put the word out there without any context.

I try again. "Did you follow me here? Are you stalking me? I'll get the authorities involved if need be. This is highly unprofessional. What on earth are you after? You can't just invade my life like this. Don't you get it? I don't want you here."

A little more aggressive than needed, perhaps, but I'm not practiced in handling conflict constructively. Dr. Joseph would be impressed I attempted to handle it at all.

Hendrix's brow furrows. "I, uh. Didn't know you'd be here, honestly."

Which has to be a load of bullshit because obviously. "You expect me to believe out of all the bars you could find yourself at in this city you end up at the one I'm at?"

His lip works itself up into a smile, and I have to remind myself not to be charmed. "Well. You did recommend Nightsky in class today."

My momentary courage deflates like Fred's inflatable plastic microphone, the one I bought him on a whim the last time we were perusing the shops in Covent Garden thinking he'd like to use it to play rap star as he's been fond of playing recently. He loved it instantly, but it only took two days before the sharp edge of a Lego poked a hole in the material and leaked all the air out.

That's me, right now. My confidence seeping out as I realize he's exactly right.

And in case I am about to try to save myself with a rant about how, just because I recommended the place doesn't mean he should go—I mean, who does that? Who actually takes someone else's unsolicited advice, on the very day the advice was given no less?—he nods his chin toward something behind him. "A few of them thought it would be fun to check it out. Get to know each other in the process. They convinced me to tag along."

My face feels hot as I turn to look, my stomach sinking as I suspect I know what I'll find. Sure enough, there's six of them, sitting round a large table on the other side of the room. Including Hendrix, that's over half the class that came out to Nightsky tonight, simply because I said I loved the place. In another situation, I'd be startled by the power of my words.

At this particular moment, however, I'm nothing short of mortified.

I turn back to the bar and press my hands to my face. They're cool against my hot skin and smell like orange since I still have the peel tucked under my thumb, out of Hendrix's sight. I'm already humiliated. He doesn't need to realize what I was drinking as well.

"Yes, right," I say because I surely need to say something. "Of course." Of course he isn't here for me. How self-centered to think otherwise. How narcissistic.

Though, he did come to this spot at the bar to order. And as the bartender sets down two negronis on the counter, my embarrassment lessens. "You came to London," I accuse. "You took my class."

"I did." He doesn't offer more. Just that twinkle in his eye and that half smile. He nods again to the table of his classmates. "Care to join us?"

I'm hit with a vivid memory of that night in Paris, the two of us sneaking away from the crowd of fellow conference-goers to debate about the best wide-angle lens, which quickly led to a discourse on the purpose of art and an instruction on how to react to a tiger in the wild. He introduced me to negronis and we'd thrown back more than a couple when he leaned in and whispered, *"My recipe is better. Come to my room, and I'll show you?"*

He never did make me that drink.

"I shouldn't," I say, declining his invitation. Even if there's a part of me that longs to sit among the bunch of them, drinking and laughing with ease, I can't begin to imagine how it would work. I wouldn't know how to *be* around them. I barely know how to be around myself.

"Shouldn't doesn't mean no." He's as much a tease now as he was then.

"But I'm saying no." It's with regret, knowing that my response will mean he leaves, and while I don't want him to stay, I don't want him to go either.

"Okay, then."

He pays the bartender, and, against my better judgement, just when he's about to grab his drink, I ask, "What happened to wildflowers in the countryside?"

It's probably telling that I remember his agenda. *Winter in the savannahs, spring wildflowers, Iceland in July.*

He turns toward me, leaning his elbow on the bar. "I had a better option."

My chest feels tight and my eyes prick suddenly. I pick up my glass and throw back the remains, which is just melted ice now. His better option is me, right? That's surely what he's saying. I'm not obtuse.

But, if he means me or if he doesn't, I don't know what to make of the statement. I don't know what to make of him. Or men in general, if I'm honest. It's why I stick to string-free sex and random hook-ups rather than relationships.

Speaking of string-free sex…

Dylan, the Thrashheads' bassist, steps up to the end of the bar and flags down the server.

"The usual?" the bartender asks, already filling up a pitcher of beer from the tap.

"The usual." Dylan notices me, and since our gaze catches, he has to acknowledge me. "Camilla," he says with that awkward sort of grin that ex-lovers share.

Could we be called lovers? "Shaggers" seems a more appropriate term to describe the quick, sordid romps we had in the back room, neither of us ever taking off more clothing than necessary, each of us rushing to orgasm like it was a race.

It's silly for him to be uncomfortable around me. We were never awkward between encounters before. Does he feel guilty for falling in love with a woman half his age and getting married, putting an end to our trysts? He shouldn't. Good for him. I hadn't expected he and I were going to turn into anything. That was the whole reason I shagged him on more than one occasion.

"You sound good tonight," I say, hoping that will ease whatever tension he's feeling.

"That's a relief. I barely can think straight with the lack of sleep."

Well, that was your fault for having twins, I want to say. But I'm polite, and so all I say is, "I'll bet."

Despite the casual air of the interaction, I'm still well aware of Hendrix and his invitations and his declarations of better options.

I'm definitely aware when he's suddenly closer, his voice low. "Are you together? Are you the cause of his lack of sleep?"

"What? No." I'm so taken aback that I'm honest without thinking. "No. Definitely not."

"But you have fucked him."

I twist my head to pin him with a scowl. "That's none of your—"

He doesn't let me finish. "I'm jealous."

I have to take a deep breath to settle the racing of my heart. To let the little lift it gives subside. To swallow the smile that very nearly surfaces, unbidden, at the thought that Hendrix is thinking about sex and me right now. What does he want from me? Am I capable of giving it? Do I want it too?

Dylan and I had a good arrangement, both of us understanding it was just sex. Could it be possible to have that with Hendrix? The bathrooms here are singles with doors that shut. We could sneak in and be out before the band started their next set. Get it out of our system, whatever this is. Would that be enough to get him to forget me and take off in search of wildflowers?

Before I can make a decision about how to respond, there's another body between us, tugging at Hendrix in a way that has spikes shooting from my skin.

"We need you, Hendrix," she says. "I have no chance at getting the history trivia without you."

She picks up the extra negroni, the one that I was sure had been ordered for me, and takes a sip. "You're right! It is good."

It's only then that she really looks at me. "Oh, it's you! I didn't realize. Of course you'd be here, since you're the one who recommended it. Still, always strange to see your teacher out in the real world."

"Just as strange to see your students," I say, though strange is a mild way of characterizing my current emotions. "Kaila, was it?"

She nods.

I only remember because of the unusual spelling of her name. She'd made sure everyone knew in her introduction. "*Kaila with an i,*" an odd bit of trivia to share, in my opinion, since if I hadn't seen it on the enrollment form, I'm pretty sure I would have wondered where exactly the i was supposed to go.

It's a fitting name, I have to admit. Creative and bubbly like she is. Based on her looks, her actions, and her resume, she's the youngest in the class. She's already working in the business, but I'm guessing she went straight from high school to an internship. She climbed the ranks quickly at the international fashion blog she works for, and I can't help being petty and wondering if she's really got talent or if she had nepotism behind her.

Hypocritical, since I only have my cushy job because of my brother. Takes one to know one, I suppose. I might not even hate her if she wasn't so obnoxiously pawing at Hendrix.

Or maybe I hate her because he ordered the negroni for her.

Or maybe I hate him for it.

Or maybe the only one I hate is me.

She takes another swallow of the bloody drink—I swear she's bragging about it—then fans herself with a flat hand. "I don't know how you're wearing a sweater. It's hot as Hades in here."

Self-consciously I tug at the cuff of my black sleeve. It's been years since I've worn anything shorter than a full-length sleeve, and I've grown used to always feeling like I'm being roasted, but I am ever aware that my outfits come across as odd at certain times of year and in certain situations.

"My temperature runs cold," I say, practiced in the excuse.

"God, I wish. I'm always a sweaty Betty. My makeup has probably melted into a mess of goo under my eyes." She glances at Hendrix, as if inviting him to say otherwise.

When he doesn't, I pick up the cue. "You look fine." I don't manage to sound very convincing. Granted, I don't really try.

It's a good enough attempt for Kaila with an i. "You should come sit with us," she offers. Her eyes are hooded, though, and as dark as her skin, and I know the only one she wants to be sitting with is Hendrix.

Yes, I've been there. And of course, the one who is jealous now is me.

"Actually, I'm leaving." I dig into my purse and find a ten pound note that I leave on the counter. It's a tip. I rarely keep a tab open, paying out after every order. I tend not to like things that keep me anchored to a place, and I avoid them at every turn.

"Oh, then." To her credit, she sounds disappointed. "We'll see you in class."

The "we" feels barbed, and I hate that I wonder about it. Wonder if Hendrix is as keen for that "we" as she is. Wonder if it's a standard routine for him to charm female photographers with negronis and his American dialect. I wonder if he'll strip her from her sleeveless romper later, if he'll bury his face between her thighs, if he'll say she tastes like tangerines, and if she'll swear it's from all the citrus drinks.

And when he moves above her in a slow, languid dance that surely mimics the stealth it takes to capture a leopard in the wild, I wonder if she'll let him keep the lights on.

"Camilla..." he says, some sort of apology in his tone, and with that single word, I'm sure he knows the color of my thoughts.

It's a relief, almost. Worrying so long about remaining hidden, to be on the brink of being seen. It's like standing at the edge of a cliff, so fearful that you'll fall that you consider just taking a step and getting it over with.

It felt like that last time with Hendrix, too.

I take a breath, and the air clears.

"See you next week," I say, blatantly shutting down whatever point he meant to make. Then I push past them both, relinquishing the space that had always been mine.

Relinquishing the man who was never mine at all.

Chapter Three

Angular: An object, outline, or shape having sharp corners, or angles.-
MoMA Glossary of Art Terms

I dump a package of pasta in the boiling water and make a mental note to take it off the burner in ten minutes. Vegetables are strewn over the cutting board, but I haven't yet got to the chopping, which means the pasta will definitely be done before the sauce. And if Freddie continues to need to show me every single one of his robot drawings with an expectation of a full art critique, there's no way I'll be getting to a salad.

Of course that's when my mobile begins to ring. A glance at the screen shows it's my brother, Edward, and God I'm tempted to let it go to voicemail.

It's not always this hard.

Or I tell myself it isn't always this hard. I'm spoiled, to be truthful. I was born into privilege and have spent most of my life basking in its advantages, but I also spent several years of my youth in a foster home where my guardians lived very much payday to payday. It was a household as short on love as it was on money, and the suffocating awfulness of those poverties is not only vivid in my memory but also branded on my skin.

So I recognize what I have is luxury. A cook and a nanny on the weekdays. Another nanny who does the cooking on Saturdays. But employees take holidays and Anwar certainly didn't plan to get sick, which is why I'm stuck both caring for my child and cooking on a Wednesday. When you add the burdens of my job and preparation for a photography course I shouldn't be teaching and the distraction of a too handsome, too charming man from my past, the tasks start to become overwhelming.

I should have ordered take away.

But I'd planned the menu when I'd given the cook the week off. I'd been very domestic about the whole thing, making sure I had the right ingredients and that each meal was well-rounded with a variety of food groups the way that responsible caretakers do all the time, all over the world, imagining Freddie's delight that I prepared something myself instead of from a ready meal, and the idea of abandoning that plan tonight made me feel inadequate. So I set out the vegetables, and I boiled the water because I *am* a good mother. I *am* a responsible caretaker.

It's being alone that's the hardest. Being the only parent. The one person who is ultimately in charge of not fucking up the most important being in my life. The task of it all would be less crushing if there was just another person to lean on every now and then. Someone to tell me I'm doing it okay. Someone to commiserate with when I've done it wrong. I don't have parents of my own to turn to since mine died when I was very young. And not only has Edward extended his time in the States, but he's also taken both his adult children with him.

I literally have no one.

Which is probably why I've spent every night this week fantasizing about Hendrix as I've fallen asleep. And it's definitely why I don't send Edward's call to voicemail, why I pick up the mobile and balance it on my shoulder with my cheek so I can have both hands free to chop the onion. Because I'm desperate to have this connection, small as it is, even in the midst of my chaos.

"The internet branding," Edward says instead of hello. Snaps, rather, and I already regret answering.

"I know, I know," I say before he goes on.

"It was due today."

"By the end of the day your time, though, right?" I glance at the clock which reminds me of the pasta, which is now boiling over. "That gives me five more hours." I drop the knife, wipe my eye with the back of my hand—onions never fail to make me cry—then rush to lift the pan of pasta from the burner.

"No, not end of day *my* time. End of day *your* time. I specifically gave that deadline so that I was sure I'd have the materials for my meeting this afternoon."

"It would have been helpful if you'd specified as such." I curse as a splash of hot water scalds the back of my hand.

"I don't usually need to specify. It's usually in my hands the day before, but you said you needed the extra time."

I had needed the extra time yesterday because a fuse had gone out on my floor at the office, and it was hours before I could even get the files loaded to examine. When I'd finally looked at them around six pm, I'd found a mistake and had to send the art back to the designer. I'd meant to go over the files as soon as I got them today.

But then Anwar got sick, and I had to leave to pick up Fred from school, and then he'd begged for the park and there was the tussle with the neighbor's rottweiler and the incident with the ice lolly and suddenly it was time to start dinner, and I hadn't opened my laptop at all.

Seeing that the water is settled, I set the pan back on the burner and leave the kitchen to grab my briefcase from where I dropped it by the front door. "I had something come up," I say as I walk, not wanting to make excuses.

"Of course. These things happen." He's not even trying to pretend he means it. Sarcasm is dripping from every syllable. "I'll just tell that to Hudson Pierce and Nathan Murphy when I sit down with them today. 'Well, I meant to have the branding graphics for the launch taking place tomorrow but, sorry. My sister said something came up.'"

He's really on a tear tonight. A man doesn't become the successful head of one of the largest media companies on the continent without having a slim intolerance for slack, and I get that. I don't expect any favors as his sister. It was favor enough that he took me in when I needed it, when he gave me the job that I certainly hadn't earned. If I have to endure his wrath for my tardiness, so be it.

Doesn't mean his words don't wake up the nag in my head. *Just like you to drop the ball. Did you expect anything different? You always fuck it up.*

My usual weapon of defense isn't helpful at the moment. *Where's the proof?* Well, the proof is that I forgot about an important deadline. That's the fucking proof.

But I have my laptop in hand now. I awkwardly open the computer as I head back to the kitchen, well aware that the pasta could boil over again if I don't keep an eye on it. "Give me half a second," I say, the mobile again propped up with my cheek. "I just need to get online and look it over. It should be a quick approval."

Unless it isn't. There's been more than one occasion that I've had to send creative back twice.

Please God don't let this be one of those times. I drop the laptop on the kitchen work top and study the image now on the screen. It's good. I mean, it's fine. It has all the elements I asked for, and the mistake from yesterday is gone.

I also suddenly have a flash of an idea, a different design altogether. More curved, less angular, a friendlier message for the alliance of three powerful companies.

It's too late to pursue the vision now. What could be has to be left at what could have been. On too many occasions, it seems. Never enough time. Never enough energy. Never enough bandwidth.

A more talented artist would have seen it earlier.

I ignore the nag and forward the file to Edward. "I sent it. You should have it shortly." Then I'm cursing again as I abandon the laptop to rescue the pasta. This time I turn down the flame when I return it to the burner.

"Got it," Edward exclaims. He becomes more compassionate with his relief. "Is everything okay over there? It's not like you to miss a deadline. Is there anything I should be concerned about?"

It's a loaded question, isn't it? Whether he means to or not, he's reminding me of all the times he's had to be concerned in the past. How often has he had to rescue me? He's been a better knight than I could ever ask for, which is another privilege, really. Especially considering that I never would ask that of him if he ever gave me the option.

There's the other reminder there too, of the time he didn't know to be concerned. How different would things be if I'd told him earlier about Frank? If I'd told my brother about the beatings and the gaslighting and the verbal abuse years before, my escape might have come at less of a cost.

But I'm not faced with a foe now as I had been then. What is there in my privileged life to concern my brother about? I can imagine how the conversation would go.

"Parenting's hard."

"Then get more help."

"It's not as easy as that."

"Should I send money?"

"That's not the support I need."

"Have you heard of an app called Tindr?"

The weight of depression is immeasurable outside of its confines. It's indescribable. There are never words to express the burden of being underneath.

It's a waste of time and energy to even discuss.

So I answer the question on the surface instead of the one he's really asking. "Just a lot going on. Shelly's on holiday, and Anwar called off sick, and Fred's a handful." I immediately feel guilty for even that. His baby is only two months old. How hard is it to run a billion dollar corporation when you never get a full night's sleep? "You know how it is."

"I do." He hesitates. I can feel him warring with himself, wondering if he should pry. "Camilla…?"

I think of Hendrix on Saturday night, the way my name sounded hanging on his tongue. I'd wanted to say more then, too. I'd wanted to say more than I'd ever said, wanted to unburden everything on him. Wanted him to hold me and tell me I was okay.

But then I'd hid, like I always do. I don't think I know any other way.

"I'm fine," I say to Edward. "Really. But if I don't get off the phone, my pasta is going to be overcooked."

He laughs, likely because the man doesn't have the slightest idea of what it takes to cook even simple spaghetti. "I'm here though. If you need anything."

"I know. Goodbye."

I throw the mobile down and resume the chopping, determined to see this meal through. I get through the rest of the onions and move to the tomatoes. The work is hypnotic—the slice of the knife through the peel and guts, the sound as it hits the board underneath. There's a satisfaction in each cut. There's permanence. A mark made that can't be undone. The most addictive form of art.

Tempting. So very tempting.

When Freddie runs in, I'm shaken from an adrenaline-filled daze. The sleeve of my long-sleeved shirt is rolled up, and I'm staring at the knife in my hand.

I blink. Horrified, I toss the utensil in the sink, as eager to have it out of my hands as I would be if it were a hot coal.

"Look at this one, Mummy. I made this one dynamite."

I laugh aloud before I take the robot drawing from him, startling us both. I turn off the burner, wipe my hands, and pick up my mobile. "Hold on one minute. Let me order dinner. Tandori sound good?"

"Extra na'an," he says. He's not disappointed in me in the least.

Chapter Four

Framing: The method by which information is included or excluded from a photograph, film, or video. A photographer or filmmaker frames an image when he or she points a camera at a subject. - *MoMA Glossary of Art Terms*

I'm quite an idiot.

I realize it when I stand in front of the class the following Saturday. Looking around, I notice most of them in jeans or relaxed wear, an appropriate choice for a weekend course, while I'm dressed in a long-sleeve trouser suit that would be better suited for the office. I can excuse my choice of attire as wanting to be professional, which is true, but the decision to apply heavier makeup and—God help me—curl my hair makes my look stand out.

It says I'm trying too hard.

And I am.

Hopefully, they believe I'm trying for them, to present myself as a suitable teacher, which again, is true, but the reality is I spent the extra time getting ready with only one student in mind. A student who I have forbidden myself from caring about.

Obviously that's going swimmingly.

It's not fair that Hendrix looks absolutely scrumptious in a pair of light khakis and a dark blue Henley. He hasn't even shaved in a couple of days, and somehow that lack of effort makes him all the more delicious.

It's quite the opposite from how he appeared in Paris. There he was clean-shaven and freshly cut, the kind of look that generally catches my eye. Paired with the slim-fit suit he'd worn for his presentation, and I was a goner.

It strikes me now that I might not have even given him a second glance if he were relaxed as he is now, yet this look is more fitting. This is who he is—rough-edged and indifferent with just a hint of wild in his eyes, despite the laid-back posture.

I memorize him in this moment, a photo snapped in my mind, framed without Kaila beside him—wasn't she a dear for saving him a seat?—so that I can study it later and fully appreciate his rugged beauty without all the noise surrounding him.

Then I put him out of my head and turn my attention fully to the class agenda.

"Every photograph should tell a story, even a portrait," I begin, and all eyes laser in on me. It's weird being the most fascinating thing in the room. Unsettling. Especially when I feel the bob of my stupid curls at each turn of my head. I feel like a performer rather than a field expert. Like I'm pretending to have something worthy to share.

It's easier when I really get into the lecture. The words flow when I'm talking about something I know, something I'm passionate about, and this particular subject is one I could spend all day on. Unfortunately, I've only allotted myself twenty minutes so I have to stick to the bare essentials, only having time to show them examples using my own work when there are so many other artists I'd love to discuss with them.

But this is a workshop, not a lecture study. I've done the math—thirteen students, a three-hour class. After I speak, that leaves them twenty minutes to get started on the activity. Then I'll have ten minutes to coach each of them individually as the rest continue to work.

I watch the clock and wrap up quickly when my limit is up. "Now it's your turn," I say, hoping I've given them enough scraps of information to make something meaningful. I divide them in three groups of three, one group of four, and send them to the hallway to take turns taking portraits of their team members.

"Why the hallway instead of in here?" one asks. Arthur who goes by the too-appropriate nickname of Arty.

My immediate reaction is to assume I've made a mistake, and I briefly question my decision along with him. The classroom is set up with backdrops and flash kits, and surely the students expect to be given time to use the equipment.

But I want to teach them photography skills that transcend the studio, and the hall outside the classroom is both quiet and magnificently lit with natural light coming through the floor-to-ceiling windows. I hadn't realized how perfect the setting was last Saturday because it had been slightly overcast when I'd come in. This morning, though, the sun was streaming in rays of gold, and I'd had to stop to catch my breath imagining the photos that could be caught there.

I'm thinking of a fancy way to explain myself, trying to figure out how to address anyone who might believe the class should be more focused on studio work when Hendrix answers simply for me. "Because of the light," he says simply. "You'll see."

Of course he's the one who understands. While everyone who registered had to have a background in art, Hendrix is the only one who had real camera experience. It's a photographer's habit to notice the light. Always measuring the luminance with the mind, at least, if not an actual photometer. It's impossible not to. Light is the basic element of photography, as necessary to the art as air and water are to the human body, and just as a person would notice when a room lacks oxygen, a photographer notices when a room lacks light.

I find I'm seeking it constantly, anchoring myself in it when it's found like a cat curling up in a bright patch of sun. Hoping one day that the light will penetrate past the layers of clothing and my mutilated skin and warm up the person inside me.

And so maybe it's the light that draws me out to the hallway with them when I'd planned to send them to work on their own while I read at my desk until it was time to meet with them one-on-one. I'd almost believe it myself if my attention was spent equally across the groups as they pose and adjust and click, click, click.

But it's hard to watch anything other than Hendrix, his expression intent as he measures angles with his eyes. I cringe imagining sitting for him, which isn't quite fair because I'd cringe sitting for anyone. But for him, especially.

I don't think about the fact that I'll have to coach him soon.

That's a lie.

I *try* not to think about it, but it's very present, like a fly trapped in the car, buzzing and buzzing as it searches the vehicle for escape, slow to take the one presented when a window is inevitably rolled down.

I'm annoyed with the buzz of Hendrix. More so than with a fly because it's my own mind that's trapped him. My own mind that refuses to shoo him out of any one of the hundred windows I've opened up to let him out.

Although I wouldn't be obsessed with him if he hadn't enrolled in my class. There. It's not my fault alone, it's his fault too. It's his fault first.

But it's my fault when he catches me watching him. And it's my fault again when I don't look away. He's too captivating, the way he studies me. His face illuminates and if I had my own camera, if I snapped right now, anyone who looked at it later would see the story. *Brutally handsome man pleased by what he sees.*

I shiver when I remember that what he sees is me.

Oh, look at that. It's time to mentor.

"All right, who's ready to discuss their work so far?" Immediately, I regret giving them the choice to step up—what if Hendrix is the first to volunteer? I can't start with him. Can't, can't, can't.

Fortunately, Salima is bouncing eagerly like Freddie when he's waited too long for the loo, and I happily attend to her first, pulling her aside in the hallway so the others in her group can continue practicing while I talk with her.

And now it's easy again. Honestly, I'm meant for one-on-one, as long as the conversation isn't centered around me. It's especially easy when there is a particular focal point for discussion and even more so when I have something worthy of saying. In this case, I have lots. Soon I've slid into the role of art critic, my tone brusque and honest with Salima and then Arty and then Karen and on down the line.

"These aren't stories, they're headshots," I say, clicking through one student's series of takes. "I feel as though I'm a casting agent. All shots looking directly at the camera, their smile fake and plastered on."

"It's not my fault Sara doesn't know how to pose."

I'm grateful I've pulled him away so that Sara doesn't hear Charlie's complaint. It's not really about her anyway. It's about him and he's being defensive.

I remind myself it's hard to accept criticism, no matter how well-meaning the critic, and take a deep breath before I speak again, more gently this time. "You have to ask for what you need if you're not getting it in the moment. It's not the job of the subject to create the art."

And so it goes, one student after another, and I discover that a few of them have a natural eye and that others are bloody awful and that most are wobbly as toddlers, still trying to adapt to the medium, but all of them are willing to learn. I see when my notes resonate, and I pivot when they don't, and each of them is quick to adjust when I watch them take a few more pics after our chat.

But now there's only one group left—three students, one of them the one I've been avoiding, and as much as I didn't want him to be first, I equally don't want to leave him for last.

I watch the three shuffle and work together, one sitting for the other two who dance around each other with their cameras. They've had more time to get shots in, and there will be a lot for me to look through, so I shouldn't delay.

Gathering myself, I call him out. "Hendrix."

He takes a second to respond, tearing himself from his hyper-focus in stages. First, he lowers his camera. Then he takes a step back. Finally, he pulls his head from Marie and looks at me. "I'm up?"

"You're up," I confirm, surprised my voice sounds as giddy as it does. Surprised that it's genuine enthusiasm.

Because I'm eager to see his work, of course. No other reason.

But when he's standing next to me, hovering over my shoulder as I flip through the pictures on his Sony A7R IV, a camera too new and too specific to portrait work to be his usual camera, I find it rather difficult to really see anything at all. My sight is overwhelmed by my other senses— the musky scent of man, the steady sound of his breaths, the heat radiating from his body that's oh, so close in proximity.

I've passed by at least a dozen shots without seeing them before I manage to force myself to blink and focus.

And now I've something new to distract me, because I've gone so far back that I've missed all the photos he took of Marie, a cheery gray-haired plump woman that one can't help but adore, and am now seeing the shots he took of Kaila. Frame after frame she fills the digital screen, and, really, she's flawless. Her skin, her coloring. The stupid little quirk of her lips.

Has he kissed those lips? Has he parted them with his tongue? Has he explored her fully with his own mouth?

I can't know from what I'm looking at, and it hurts to wonder, but it hurts even more to hope that he hasn't so I lean into the pain and accept that he probably has. And why wouldn't her lips quirk up at the attention of her lover? Why wouldn't she look radiant in his presence?

Except that's not her, I realize when I study further. That's the photographer making her glow. That's Hendrix's ability to capture the light.

Once I see his talent, I'm able to see past the subject. I knew he was good before, of course. I've pored over many of his nature shoots online late at night since our tryst in the autumn, enough to understand his style, and I'm sure I could correctly identify his work out of dozens of others.

I see that style here in the framing and the angles and the concept. But beyond the technique, there is something missing, something I can't identify.

"What's the story?" If he can't articulate it, that will be the reason I can't find it.

"A bright, young ambitious girl nervous under the scrutiny of someone she admires."

I frown at his answer, unwittingly. I'm both impressed and annoyed that he's that aware of his subject. "Yes, I suppose it would make her nervous to be photographed by the man she's crushing on."

Is my envy evident? It's nonsense jealousy, wanting his attention and not wanting it all-at-once. I'm sure I confuse him. I'm confused myself.

"I was talking about her teacher."

Now I'm confused by him. I look up questioningly, prompting an explanation.

"She knew you were watching. Of course she was preoccupied wondering what you were thinking. What you observed."

I actually laugh. The man is not as self-aware as I thought. "She's preoccupied with you, not me. Trust a woman to know."

"Well, then," he says with a shrug, "I guess I was confusing her story with mine."

A strange spiraling emotion takes me over, tightening my chest as it wraps around me, leaving me warm as it slithers down. I'm embarrassed and thrown. What's his motive? He can't be speaking from a place of sincerity. And also, dammit, he saw me watching, and now I suddenly want to bury my head in a hole.

I throw my gaze back to the screen so he doesn't see the flush in my face and take the moment to regroup. "It's the right story," I say, as though he hadn't just shot an arrow to my heart. "It doesn't matter exactly who it was who had her flustered. The fact remains that she is pleasantly uneasy. I can see that clearly." It's most evident in the series of shots, which is not a lesson I have planned to teach for another couple of weeks. Leave it to Hendrix to tackle assignments in advance.

I stop at a particularly well-composed frame. Technically, it's perfect, but it's not right. I mean, it's head and shoulders above anyone else I've critiqued today, which is what makes it all the more frustrating to not be able to put a finger on the flaw. There is agony in the "almost." More so than when a mark is missed entirely. I'd rather the miss any day. To be so close to the goal and miss it by a hair? That's a kind of torment that haunts.

It makes me all the more eager to figure out the fix, not just because it's Hendrix who is facing this potential torment. I would be equally motivated if it were any of my students, but also, admittedly, this torment will also haunt me if not resolved *because* it is Hendrix.

I twist my lips, studying, thinking. I flip through the last images. I flip back. "I need to see something," I say. Without waiting for his response, I march through the classroom door—propped open since it's the kind that automatically locks when shut—to the computer at my desk. I wiggle the mouse to wake it up, type the title of the photo I'm looking for in the browser search bar, and hit enter.

It isn't until the image is full on the screen and he leans in to look with me that I realize that he followed me in here. That I realize that we're practically alone. That I realize that I've made an awesome mistake.

My heart quickens its pace.

"Leopard, sleeping," he says, repeating the name of the photo before us. "That one won me the BWPA. Almost four years ago now. Flattered you knew it by name."

Sure, he's flattered. I'm...well, I'm a bit embarrassed, of course, but not as badly as I would have imagined I'd be. I'd forgotten that about him, that he has a way of easing me like a fragrant balm against sliced skin.

"It's worthy of the award, though not my favorite." I'm not sure why I'm being so honest. Probably because I've gone completely nutters and have lost all control.

"And which one is that? Your favorite." He's closer now, his head lowered so that I can feel his exhale at the side of my cheek.

"Elephant playing in black and white," I admit.

"That one is a favorite of mine as well."

As it should be. I'd be beside myself cocky if I'd taken that shot or anything near it. It's complete magic how he captured the animal spouting water from its trunk at its companion, the droplets of water catching the sun like diamonds. It's playful and charming and poignant, capturing a kinship between two animals that is rarely caught among humans. Or perhaps it's that I have been so rarely playful myself.

I've spent endless hours with it, and still, every time I see it something blooms inside me.

But I didn't rush in here to fawn over his art.

I nod toward the screen. "This is nearly identical to that photo of Kaila."

"I'm not sure she'd appreciate being compared to a wild animal, but go on."

"Not the leopard itself," I sigh. "The composition. The angle, the way you've framed it, the direction of the light. Do you see it?" It's his style epitomized in both shots.

"Are you worried I plagiarized myself? I promise I'm not going to issue a complaint."

I shoot him a look that says *would you please understand me?* Sometimes I find that works as well as explaining myself, if not better.

This time it seems to do the trick. "All right, I see what you're seeing," he says. "This shot is much better than any on that camera you're holding though."

Exactly my point. "So what's the difference?" I've had mentors ask me similar questions. I always assumed they knew the answer when they asked and just wanted me to find it for myself, but now I wonder if they just realized the only person who can really say what's missing from a piece when it's that near perfection is the person who sees it best of all, the person who saw it from scratch before it was a moment or a story or art. When it was raw and living.

Hendrix straightens, and I follow like I'm tied to him with an invisible string because I know he knows the answer, and I'm eager to have the mystery solved.

"Easy," he says. "My subject today wasn't the most fascinating thing in the vicinity."

It's a loaded statement, one that has me rejoicing and melting and panicking all at the same time. It's a relief that he doesn't like that twit, which isn't a fair thing to call her at all since she has not demonstrated any reason to be labeled as such except to exist. And it's exactly what was missing from the photo. It's a breakthrough when a person can identify the flaw so succinctly, and always deserves to be acknowledged as such.

Which makes me want to give him a high five or a fist bump or whatever it is that's the current way to express congratulations. Makes me feel almost playful enough to do so.

But his answer was also pointed, and while I'm quick to self-doubt, I'm perceptive enough to know what he's saying, and now I can no longer cling to any confusion about why he took this class. He's here for me. He took this class for me.

"Camilla…" It's the same way he said my name the other night at the bar, an invitation and a warning that whatever follows will be hard for me to hear. A pause to let me decide if I can bear it.

Frankly, I'm not sure that I can. It's a lot to process. And the clock is ticking in the back of my head. Two more students to get through. No time to acknowledge this. No desire to deal.

"I have to get back to the others," I say dismissively. I hand him his camera and, like I did at Nightsky, I head for the door.

He follows this time, though. Because that's where he's supposed to go, not because he's chasing after me, yet it feels like being chased, and while I wanted to get away from him that night, I don't feel that desperation today. Turns out I sort of like the feeling of being chased, a surprise to me since I dreaded anytime Frank came after me. Different circumstances, of course. Frank rewarded me with beatings when I was caught, convincing me I deserved it because how dare I run? It would be understandable if I had permanent PTSD from it. I definitely did for quite some time. Perhaps that's why I'm always running from lovers who I am absolutely sure will not follow.

Hendrix, though.

Is it possible I like that he's come for me? Is it possible that I could enjoy what would be waiting if he caught me? Is it possible that I could try?

I'm not sure. There's a hopeful buoyancy in my limbs, though, as I conference with the last two, and a smile dresses my face as I wrap up the class and give the homework for the week. I'm nervous for the class to end, knowing Hendrix will surely approach me, but I'm excited too.

Which is why I'm crushed when he doesn't stay after to talk. He lingers to gather his things, letting everyone else leave ahead of him, but then he slings his camera bag over his shoulder and starts for the door, a door that will lock as soon as it swings shut behind him, and he won't be able to come back in, and I'm so scared by that metaphor that I call out after him. "Hendrix!"

He turns without hesitation, his brown eyes warm like melted chocolate. "Yes?" he says, and he doesn't sound at all annoyed. Rather he sounds as desperate and anxious as I am, and the pressure to say the right thing is there, pressing against my trachea as if to block the possibility of words in case they are the wrong ones.

"I…" God, what are the right ones? I know how to seduce a man, but I don't know what this is, and I sure as hell don't know how to do it.

But Hendrix does, and like I coached the class today, he coaches me. "Say it, Camilla. Say what you want, whatever it is. Big or small."

I close one eye, like I do when I'm behind the camera, and zero in on the shot, barely breathing in case I lose it. Then I shoot. "I find you the most fascinating thing in the vicinity too."

He smiles and nods, as though he already knew, before I even did, and maybe he really did because I said it, and I mean it, and he isn't surprised. His smile fades now, and he grows somber, and I brace myself for the seriousness of what he's about to say. "Dinner tonight?"

I laugh, the tension relieved by his simple request. Or not so simple since it's not the easiest thing for me to agree to on most occasions, but it's so much easier than whatever else I thought he might say, which is silly because what could he say that would be so frightening?

Actually, a lot.

But all he's asked for is this, and wanting to live my life, I tell him yes.

Chapter Five

Concentric: Two or more things having a common center. - *MoMA Glossary of Art Terms*

The perfect photo creates a memory.

It's the same the other way around. The most important moments, the ones that feel crafted and composed and perfect, those are the ones that stick with you. A lifetime is a collection of those moments, collected like snapshots in the scrapbook of your mind.

There are a lot of photos in my past that I don't like to look at, entire albums of memories that I've stored away on shelves. They're dusty and faded now, and even when I do pull them out to look at, I'm not sure anymore that what I'm looking at is accurate. They're too yellowed, like photos from the past, the kind taken on Kodak paper that wasn't meant to endure through time.

The evening with Hendrix, seven incredible hours, fills a memory book all on its own. Like so many others, I try not to look at that one very often. I sneak it out on occasion, usually in the dark when Freddie's asleep and the house is quiet, when the presence of the album flashes like a neon sign in the dark. I regret it every time, tucking it back on its shelf in the morning, promising not to touch it again. Sometimes that promise lasts a week or two. Sometimes I don't make it more than a day.

The problem with looking at this particular album is how happy it makes me feel. Sunshine peeking through the trees on Tarr Steps kind of happy, which, in my opinion, is the ultimate pinnacle of happiness. That's what the night was like last autumn.

It's funny how sometimes joy can hurt as much as pain. Because it's fleeting, perhaps. Because even when you're in the middle of it, you're aware that it won't last. It's a bubble of a feeling, buoyant and light and free. The kind of feeling you want to chase after, even knowing that once it's caught it will pop.

And, oh, that pop is always such a surprise. Where once there was something and now it's completely gone.

In the space of time between class and my date with Hendrix—no, not date, I refuse to call it that when it's merely a meal we'll be sharing—before I get fussy over my attempt to get ready, I allow myself to take the album out and look at it in the daylight. It's heavier than I remember, divided into four distinct series, each containing their own arc, and each individual photo memory is as vivid and bright as the day it was taken.

I wear a smirk as I study the first series. I'd been part of the final conference event of the evening, a panel discussing the current trends of photography in the corporate field. I'd been nervous about the whole thing and needed a drink when it was all over, but in the end I'd been pleased with my contributions, pleased enough to accept the invitation to go to a local restaurant with the other panelists and a group of conference attendees.

I'm not sure how Hendrix got in the mix. He'd known one of the speakers or had nothing better to do with his night and had popped into the panel out of curiosity. However it happened, I found myself seated next to him at one of the several tables our group occupied, and with the buzz of the event being over and a job well done, along with a dirty martini already in my system, somehow idle conversation among many turned into a heated discussion between just the two of us.

"Of course branding should be considered art!" My exclamation came in response to his suggestion that graphic design didn't have a place in the community. "There is just as much sweat, blood, and tears invested in the pieces that come across my desk as there are on any of the prints hanging in the Foam. More so even, considering what's on the line for the designs if they don't do the right job."

"But that's just the thing," he protested. "They have different goals. Branding is meant to get people to spend. Art is for people to enlighten and enjoy."

"As if you aren't looking for a payday when you're trekking through the wilderness. There's a reason they call it a money shot."

"Of course I'm hoping to get paid, but the shot is the end product for the consumer. It's not a bridge to something else."

"Isn't it?" I fired back, enjoying the debate. "When National Geographic uses one of your photos, they're expecting it to draw people into the accompanying article. Exactly what branding is meant to do, except that branding is honest about it. And more practical. It should be rewarded."

"It *is* rewarded. With a paycheck."

"It should be rewarded in the galleries too, as far as I'm concerned. It's an outdated notion that a creation is either profitable or it's art. I promise you, it can be both."

He paused then, studying me before a grin appeared, the first full grin I'd seen from him, and it was electrifying. Literally. I still remember the shock that jolted through me at the sight of it. "It can be both," he repeated, as though testing out the idea.

"It most definitely can." I smiled back, and yes, I was flirting. The conversation had moved from a discussion about something I found interesting with a stranger to a discussion about something with a stranger I found interesting. That didn't happen very often for me. I found a man I was attracted to easily enough, but I was never interested beyond the endgame. The conversation was the branded design leading to the eventual fuck.

With Hendrix, though, I was interested in being in the moment. I was interested in more than what he had hidden under his clothes. I was also interested in what he had hidden in his brain. He was engaging and arresting, and I was undeniably charmed.

He was too, it seemed. It was in his eyes, in the tilt of his head. In the words that came next from his mouth. "Want to discuss it over a drink in the lounge where it's quieter?"

Maybe I hemmed and hawed about it a bit before saying yes, but it was already decided in my mind. I knew that I would spend every last second of the night with him, whatever it took, even if it meant only the drinks and the banter. Even if it meant accompanying him to his room. I remember knowing that. I don't remember the details of actually moving from this sequence to the next, but I do remember knowing I was all in for the night.

Mostly, I remember the warm glow of happiness. He made me smile.

The next series of memories picks up in a dark corner of the lounge, the rest of our group abandoned along with my dirty martinis. Instead, he'd ordered negronis for us both, and I was instantly in love. With the drink, not the man.

Well. The man too.

It seems naïve to say that I could use such a bold word to describe my enamorment so quickly and be certain that it was accurate, but I am certain. I'm not romantic about it. I don't pretend to believe that he would feel the same or that I would want him to feel the same or that it would ever be more than just that one evening together. I only know that sometime between the first sip of the Italian cocktail and when Hendrix paid the tab, I fell in love.

It might have been when he confessed that he still carried a film camera with him on location along with his digital or when he thoughtfully traced across the back of the hand I'd rested on my lap like he was painting it into being with his thumb. I'd definitely realized it by the time he was describing what it was like to burrow in a forest and hide for hours at a time waiting to capture a shot of an elusive lynx.

"It's a constant adjustment of position," he said. "Always subtle so as not to disturb the environment. Just enough to wake up the limb that's fallen asleep in the previous position."

"That sounds like it takes tenacity." I'd been in awe. I wasn't a big fidgeter, but I certainly wasn't great at being still. Except, perhaps, when he spoke.

"Patience is probably one of my strengths." His cheeks might have got red at that. It was hard to tell in the dim light of our corner, but he was humble enough about it that I imagined the heat in his face at the self-recognition. "It's worth it though. Waiting and waiting and waiting and sure you're going to be disappointed and then suddenly, there it is—a creature wild and uninhibited and free. And that specific animal has likely never been seen by another human. It's deeply profound and quite personal. I don't usually talk about it, to be honest."

My first impulse was to say he didn't need to talk about it with me then—it's the instinct I've learned, to detach myself from another's possible regret. But he and I were already past that, and I wanted to linger in the intimacy of his sharing. The feeling I got when I realized I'd been in his confidence. "That sounds beautiful," I said, my voice hushed as though I were in the forest with him.

"It's the most I feel alive. When I'm face-to-face with something fierce and feral. Not that everything I photograph is dangerous by any means. In fact, most animals I shoot aren't. I photograph a lot of owls, for example—they're so expressive, I can't help myself. But the fierce ones have the most impact. The lions. The tigers on the prowl. The bear defending its cub. The hippos—any encounter with a hippo is memorable. The wolves."

"What's your favorite of them all?" I asked, my gaze darting to his lips.

"Of all the wild animals I've encountered?" His tone said I'd asked him an impossible question, and yet he didn't hesitate after my nod. "You."

I left for the lavatory then, and he followed after me, which I had hoped he would do. This series of memories is filthy and frenetic—my trousers pooled on the floor around my ankles, my hands braced on the sink, the rip of the condom packaging, the slapping of his thighs against mine as his cock pounded rhythmically into me.

The end of this sequence would normally be where I walked away. There hadn't been a man since Frank that hadn't received a goodnight from me seconds after the disposal of the condom.

That wasn't the case with Hendrix. When he finished zipping up his slacks, he turned me around and pressed his forehead against mine. "This can't be all I have of you," he pleaded, as though he suspected my usual habit to run. "Please, please let me have more."

I wondered if that was his prayer in the rainforest, when after waiting for most of the day for something incredible to show itself, a jaguar crept into view only to immediately turn and flee at an accidental sound made by Hendrix in his excitement to capture the animal on camera.

It wasn't because he sounded so desperate that I agreed. It was because I echoed his prayer. I not only wanted more of him, I wanted more of me. The witty, confident me that I was with him. The me that he saw me to be. Were they one and the same? I wasn't sure, but I wanted them to be. And he was the reason I'd seen the possibility.

I wanted them to be so much that I didn't think about what I was agreeing to, not as we walked hand-in-hand to his hotel, not as I followed him up the narrow staircase, not as he slid the key into the lock—one of those old-fashioned kinds, not the plastic keycard sort—not as he pulled me past the threshold and into his arms.

My lips shifted against his easily that time. The first kiss back in the restaurant lav had been awkward with its greediness, our teeth clacking and our tongues in the way. In his room, the kiss was like slow dancing, languid and in sync, and though I was not often very big on kissing, I could have stayed in that embrace, our mouths locked, for hours.

But of course there'd be more than kissing, and it wasn't until we were on his bed and his hands reached for the buttons of my long-sleeve blouse that I began to panic.

I put a hand up to stop him, and before he could ask for an explanation, I cupped my palm over the thick bulge in his crotch, which turned out to be an effective distraction for all of about five minutes. Soon enough, he was fumbling with the buttons once more.

This time putting up a hand wasn't enough. "Could we…" I'd never stumbled on this request before. I didn't know why it was so hard to voice it this time. "Do you mind if we keep most of our clothes on?"

He let go of my shirttail and cupped my face, pulling me in for a searing kiss. "Whatever you need," he said, and I knew he meant it. He had the patience of a wildlife photographer, after all. "Just, you should know how badly I want to touch you."

I could have let it go at that. Skin-to-skin during sex is a beautiful thing, definitely heightens the intimacy, but since beautiful and intimate are not ever my objective, I am apt to not care about the absence.

Most men don't care either once they've got their cock inside me. It's helpful in this that they tend to have a one-track mind.

But there with Hendrix, pressed up against him with my clothes on and still feeling miles away from satisfaction, it was harder to ignore his desires. His desires were my desires, deep and desperate and greedy.

I glanced across the room at the windows, covered with blackout curtains. The lamps around the room were already all turned off save the one on the nightstand. An excited sort of anxiety tightened around my chest, gripping tighter as the urge to speak increased, like a failsafe my body had set up in case of stupid decisions like this one, a warning that it would shut down my ability to breathe before it let me proceed.

But Hendrix made me feel brave. Because I was in love with him. Because I was in love with the person he saw when he looked at me. Because in that moment, I was happy.

"Turn off the light?" It was a question because I was uncertain about what I was doing, but he answered like it was meant for him to answer.

"I can do that if you prefer."

I didn't know what I preferred. I knew what was necessary because now that the idea was in my head, I needed to be naked against him as surely as I needed to not be seen. So I said, "Yes. Please."

It was torture just to lose his presence long enough for him to roll over and reach for the lamp. He flipped the switch, and we were pitched into the security of darkness. Pretty solid darkness, too. Those blackout curtains earned their name.

It was more eagerness than nerves that had me fumbling with the buttons of my shirt. Then I was fumbling with his buttons, and quickly we were both bare, top to bottom, wearing nothing but the dark.

And God, had touch always felt that magnificent? Like a favorite blanket fresh from the dryer, I wanted every part of my skin wrapped with his. I can still feel that want with an embarrassing degree of lust. Can still feel the desire to explore every inch of his nudity with the tips of my fingers.

I didn't indulge, of course. Those kinds of liberties are expected to be exchanged in kind in those situations, and I couldn't endure much in return. I did allow him to fondle my breasts, let him tease my nipples to sharp peaks. Allowed my own palms to sweep up and down the sculptured landscape of his chest.

When it seemed the touching might progress to more wandering, I distracted him yet again. "I have a condom in my purse." It was going to be hard to find in the darkness, but I was up for the challenge.

"I have one. Grabbed it from my wallet before my pants came off."

What a gorgeous man. Sincerely. Perfection.

Also a mite alarming that he'd had more than one condom stashed away, but I wasn't about to get hung up on his possible sexual habits when I was the benefactor, and who was I to judge anyway?

The series of photo memories that play out from here aren't necessarily my favorite of the album, but they are the ones I look at the most often. Usually with my eyes shut tight and my hand buried between my legs. It's an absolutely wicked arc of a story they tell, provocative and obscene with the way he drilled into me, the way he ground his hips against mine. The delicious drag of his cock moving in and out and in and out. It was slower than the frenetic pace from the bathroom earlier, but still a tempo that had us soon sweating.

The sticky feel of his body pressed to mine may have been the trigger for my first orgasm. Bless the man, I had three total. Three earth-shattering Os that each wrecked me in its own beautiful way.

I'm not sure I would have had any of them at all if I hadn't been able to relax with him as I did. I tend to be overly tense with my clothes off, even in the darkness, but the fear that Hendrix's hands might roam while we fucked was quickly eliminated when he drew my arms over my head and threaded his fingers through mine.

Strange how connected to a person you can feel just by having your hands laced.

His cock inside me, too, but our hands...maybe because it was exactly what I needed at the moment, I'm not sure. Whatever the reason, it's our locked hands that I focus on the most whenever I look back.

The series ends with his collapse on the bed next to me, my cheek pressed against his chest as his breathing evened out and grew deeper, his arm wrapped loosely around my waist. I don't ever look at the sequence of events that followed—the part where he fell asleep, the part where I swallowed back a sob, the part where I stealthily rolled from his arms and groped around in the dark to find my clothes and then dress and then leave that me—*his* me—behind with him. There's a story in those memories too, but I've done my best to forget them. And today when I'd do best to remember why I snuck out, why I couldn't possibly stay, why there is no way on God's green earth that it could happen again, I still can't bring myself to acknowledge them.

Maybe I avoid that story because it's too hard to bear.

More likely I avoid it because it's so easy for me to see it ending another way.

Chapter Six

Juxtaposition: An act of placing things close together or side by side for comparison or contrast. - *MoMA Glossary of Art Terms*

It was a moment of weakness to agree to dinner, but at least I had sense enough to insist that I'd meet Hendrix at the restaurant instead of letting him pick me up. It makes it easier to lie to myself about what this is, why I said yes. It's a fact-finding mission. That's all. Not a date. Not an encounter with expectations beyond the meal. Not an opportunity to spend time with someone I am really, really fond of.

He picked well for the location, too. It's more pub than restaurant, which keeps it casual and helps enforce my lie. Since it's not one of those fancy places with rules about only complete parties being seated, he's already at our table when I arrive. He sees me when I'm still across the room, watches as I approach with keen eyes and barely any movement. I know in my gut that this is exactly the way he looks when he sits in wait for his elusive wild creatures to appear.

It makes my breath catch, the awareness that he's waiting for me with that depth of perseverance.

He stands when I reach him, but he's wise enough not to try to greet me with any physical connection. I find that both admirable and disappointing.

"You're ravishing," he says after his gaze takes in my gray ruffle blouse (long-sleeve, of course) and my black cigarette pants. His voice is reverent, as though he's awed by the sight of me. As though he still sees me as that woman I became with him.

Talk like that will be my undoing.

"This is not a date," I say, an attempt to plant myself on firm ground.

His lip twitches like it's fighting a smile. "Of course not."

I'm not reassured. But I sit anyway. He follows suit.

So. This is really happening.

"I'm not late," I say, more of a statement than a question. I know I've arrived right on time. I planned it so, but as much as I despise small talk, I need something to say and it's the first thing that comes to mind.

"No. I'm early." He's still looking at me with that expression of wonder that has me feeling all sorts of wrecked inside, and fuck it, I can't sit here if he's going to keep this up.

"Stop." I can't even look in his direction. His gaze is like a studio lamp, too bright to look directly at. "Stop looking at me that way."

"What way?"

I'm annoyed by his feigned innocence. "Like you're amazed by my presence." I feel uncomfortable as soon as I've called him out. Then it occurs to me that maybe his awe is in the fact that I showed up. "You didn't honestly think I might ghost, did you?"

He gives a half-shrug. "It crossed my mind."

My chest loosens. That's a much more tolerable reason for awe than the alternative. "Please. I said I'd be here, and so I am. I'm not scared of you."

"Yes, you are."

And just like that, I'm tight and tense again. It's not fair that he knows that. It's hard enough being the one afraid.

As though he senses my alarm, he adds, "If it makes you feel any better, I'm scared of you too."

"Bollocks. As if I'm to believe that after all the adventures you've been on. It's unlikely you're scared of anything."

He folds his arms and leans them on the table between us, pitching him forward. "Now that is awfully presumptuous. Just because I'm out facing the fear doesn't mean I don't feel it. Believe me, I feel it quite intensely."

"Then why do what you do?"

"Maybe I like being scared." His tone doesn't sound like he's trying to be a tease, rather that he's trying to figure it out for himself. "Maybe it makes me feel alive. Maybe it's because the truly scary things tend to bring the biggest reward."

Well, then. We're far from the shallow now, aren't we? Is it too late to run?

Fortunately, Hendrix decides I need a reprieve. "How about I go order? Do you know what you want?"

I'm so eager for him to be gone, for me to have a moment to regroup that I don't even bother with the menu. "Fish and chips are fine." Greasier than I usually go for, but it's an item I'm sure they'll have.

"And to drink?"

"You choose." It instantly feels too personal for some reason, but it's been said and even the "Whatever" I add doesn't diminish the intimacy.

But it's enough to send him on his way, and with him gone, I can breathe. In, out. In, out.

And now that I can think again, I miss him.

I contain multitudes. Not just contradicting myself from day-to-day but from minute-to-minute. I don't want to be here, in this situation, feeling this unmoored. And, also, there's nowhere else I'd rather be.

It's better when he returns. Like his absence has reset the conversation, and we start again, on surer footing when he asks my opinion on the Gupta exhibition at the TPG. We quickly slip into that familiar banter I remember. It's easy to discuss art and philosophy while we sip contessas, a variation on the classic negroni, I learn, when Hendrix explains all of his favorite varieties of the Italian cocktail.

I learn other things too. Silly, trivial things. That his favorite movie is Kurosawa's Ikiru. That Hendrix is a family name and not a tribute to the famed guitarist. The evening is reminiscent of the first series from our first night together—engaging dialogue, passionate opinions. Nothing too personal. Nothing too hard. And all underscored by that happy glow of feeling at home with someone. If I'd wondered at all that our ability to connect had been a one-time thing, I now know definitively that it was not. Hendrix Reid fits me tonight as well as he did last autumn. Like tailor-made trousers. Like a memory card in my Nikon D6. Like the key in the lock of his hotel room in Paris.

While it's both of us directing the turns of conversation equally, I avoid the questions that I have told myself are my reason for being here. Not because I suddenly don't want the answers but because I suspect those will be harder subjects to negotiate. For me, anyway. Perhaps for him too.

It's not until we're on our third drink and I'm pushing away the scraps of my meal that the shift occurs. It's my fault because I bring up Freddie. Nothing major, just an anecdote that relates to our discussion on conceptual inspiration, but speaking his name at all opens a door to more personal topics, and exactly as contradictory as I was earlier, I'm not sure if I want to cross that threshold or not.

Hendrix makes his own decision and steps in before me. "Are you interested in more children?"

"No," I say quickly. Too quickly so it reads as untrue, and it is, which feels very unscrupulous. I might not be forthright when it comes to this man, but I haven't been outright dishonest. I don't like the taste of the dishonesty now.

I take a sip of my drink, and I amend. "Well. I did."

"What made you change your mind?"

I almost laugh. Isn't it obvious? "I'm too old now."

"No. You're not."

I circle my neck, stretching the tendons that have tightened there. "I might be," I say, and that's honest. For some reason it's easier to just assume that I am. The possibility that the season hasn't passed is way too fragile of a thing to hold in my head. "Biologically, I might be done. Once a woman hits thirty-five...it's harder."

He nods in acceptance, as though my answer has anything to do with him. "Then you adopt," he offers.

I've actually considered it. Especially when Fred was younger, and I dreamed of having another for him to play with. And also I've considered it recently. Now that he's six and the age difference between him and a new sibling would be the same as the age difference between me and Edward.

There's only one thing that stops me. "I don't want to do it alone again. I can afford it, I know. I could hire the help. I believe, I think, that a parent doesn't need to be omnipresent to do a good job. But it's lonely. To not have someone invested as much as you are. To have to wonder and worry and dream all on your own. I hadn't planned to parent alone the first time. I don't think I can do it willingly."

"Then don't do it alone."

Now I do laugh. "Just poof a partner into being? It takes time to do the whole dating thing. Then the engagement. The marriage. There's an order to it. Even if I found the right man today, it would take probably more time than I have, especially since I won't be giving my heart out easily this time."

He does that arms on the table lean, bringing him centimeters closer to me. "Fuck the traditional order. Do it however you want. Find the guy, decide to be parents together, take your time to see if it turns into more."

Even fucking the order, there are still flaws in his idea. Finding a guy who wants to partner in parenting, finding a guy at all.

Unless he's offering to be the guy.

And I'm suddenly hopeful and terrified that he is. The bubble is on the verge of popping and I'm not ready.

Oh, God. What am I doing?

"Why did you come here?" I blurt it out, out of nowhere. Because it's time. Because I need to know. "Why did you enroll in my class, out of all the classes you could take in the world? And don't give me some bullshit about wanting to broaden your skills because that doesn't answer why me. And after seven months with no word between us, why now?"

"You were the one who snuck out without leaving any way to contact you."

"That's the universal code for this is only a one-night stand."

"Which is why it took me seven and a half months to show up."

He's intense when he's serious. Intense and vulnerably accurate. I'd held back adding the half to our months apart because I didn't want to give away that I've counted the time, but he's put it out there for me to see it of him. Even if he's scared, he's so much braver than I. I'm too scared even to respond.

Boldly, he reaches across the table to stroke my hand with his thumb, the way he did that other night. I should pull it away. This series cannot lead to the same series now as it did then.

But he's pinned me in place with the simple power of his touch, and like an animal frightened by a possible predator, I remain in place.

While I stare at the path his thumb takes, I can feel him staring at me. "I was trying to honor your choice," he says softly, a whisper really. "I really was, Camilla, but I couldn't do it anymore. I couldn't keep pretending that there was anything in the world that interested me besides you."

Oh my.

To be wanted. To be wanted enough to be pursued. I haven't entertained those possibilities in a very long time. Haven't even entertained the fantasy. It's too ludicrous when I feel so unworthy of that kind of wanting.

But I'm trying to look at the proof, and the proof is in his words. The proof is that he's here. And for a handful of seconds I consider what could become of that.

The considering doesn't go too far before I remember that the vulnerability he's offering has to be met in kind for it to work.

And I can't be that naked, in any sense of the word. Not for Hendrix. Not for anyone.

I pull my hand away abruptly. "I'm sorry, I don't feel the same." The bitter taste of deceit returns. Before I'm tempted to wash it down with truth, I stand. "I think it would be best that we call it a night."

I'm heading out the door before he can stop me, confident that he won't follow. He knows there's no use chasing after the animal he's after. He knows it's best to lie in wait.

Outside, I pull up the Uber app as soon as I realize that catching a taxi in this part of town on a Saturday night is not happening. Car ordered, I lean against the stone exterior of the pub and will myself not to cry.

Next thing I know, Hendrix is standing next to me. Because I'm not an animal, I'm a woman, and why would he stay in the pub when the bill was already paid and I'd left?

And if he was the type of man to follow me to London, he certainly wouldn't be the type of man to leave me brooding in peace.

I sigh when I see him, a big, desperate, anguished sigh. "I can't," I say. Because I can't. I can't anything with him. I can't even with myself.

"I know," he says calmly. "So let me." With his hands in his pockets, he steps in, so close that I can't look in his eyes. So close that we're almost touching. It feels like we're touching, even though there's not a part of me in contact with him. "I know you don't mean what you said in there. I know that you feel something. And I know that, for whatever reason, you aren't able to let that keep you from walking away right now."

His tone is patient. His words, given as a gift, not to persuade but to soothe. And the electricity bouncing between us...would it send mixed messages if I let him take me in the alley for a quickie?

It's sad that that's where my mind goes, when sex is already part of my routine and what he's offering is something so much more uncommon in my life. Happiness. Not the daily small joys I have naturally with Freddie, but the kind that come from being chosen. Is that why I run from it? Because it's too foreign? Too unknown?

Probably that, and also it's hard to trust something so intangible. Sex is easy in comparison. It's concrete. It has a clear objective. It has a clear end.

Of course, with what he's said, with the declaration of his interest, sex can't just be sex anymore. It will forever after be more.

So I bite my lip so I don't suggest it. I breathe in his scent, a mix of sandalwood and musk. I take a snapshot for my memory book. I don't lean forward to press my forehead against his chin. When he speaks again, I listen.

"I need you to know that I'm here," he says. "Afraid because of how much I want you. Willing to wait for any scrap of you that you're able to give. If this is all I get, if this is all I *ever* get, it will still have been worth it."

He goes then, walking in the direction of the tube, without so much as the barest brush of his body against mine.

I watch him leave, my heart heavy and full, the camera behind my eyes click, click, clicking until he's just a blur disappearing in the distance.

Chapter Seven

Proportion: Refers to the harmonious relation of parts to each other or to the whole. - *MoMA Glossary of Art Terms*

"You said we'd go swimming." Fred tugs at my arm as he attempts to pull me in the direction he believes goes to his uncle's house.

"We will go swimming," I promise. Edward has a pool on his ground level, and though he's still in the States, we often slip over to use it. I'll only don a costume if we're alone, and Freddie's much too young to be swimming without someone ready to jump in after him if need be so my brother's mansion across from Regent's has become our swim spot. I've even taken to leaving our costumes there to make the journey less of a hassle.

Though I do intend to keep the Sunday plans I made with my son, there's another thing on my agenda as well. "Remember I said we were going to the park first?"

"But this is the boring part of the park." He kicks at the walk with the toe of his shoe. I'm lucky this is his version of a tantrum, he's such a well-behaved kid. "Do we have to look at weird art again?"

That was my bad. The last event I dragged him to at this park was the Frieze art fair. I learned too late that he'd been maybe a little too young to fully appreciate it. I'm hoping today's art will be of more interest to him. "It's a little weird," I confess. "I think it will be fun too."

He frowns as he kicks the walk again. "But will it be as fun as swimming?"

Swimming, for him, involves splashing half the water out of the pool, shrieking in glee, and heaving toys to and fro until he's exhausted. This won't involve any of those things. I consider lying, but I've committed to a parenting style that embraces honesty as much as possible, so I toss the idea aside and settle for the truth. "Probably not quite as fun. We won't stay long, okay?"

He heaves a sigh that seems awfully large for his little body. "Okay."

I survey the horizon, pinpointing my destination. With a twinge of guilt, I tow him toward the performers ahead of us. I haven't been completely transparent, hiding my motives for this part of our trek. What am I supposed to tell a six-year-old boy, though, when I can't fully explain my reasons even to myself?

I should take that as a sign that this particular adventure is better avoided, but here we are, my child and me with my multitudes standing in front of the living statue competition against all better reasoning.

Fortunately, Fred is mesmerized. "Are they...?" He's hesitant to make his guess out loud, understandably since the performers are that good. "Are those real people?"

"They are. Isn't it incredible?" Together we walk closer toward one of the "statues," a man covered head to toe in bronze seated on a park bench and frozen in a pose. He's so still, it takes me a minute to discern he's actually breathing.

Fred clings next to me, suddenly intimidated. "He doesn't get to move at all?"

"Well, he won't stay like that forever, but he'll certainly stay for long enough that it grows uncomfortable. Can you imagine sitting that still?"

There's a part of me that can imagine it. The part of me that finds discomfort so familiar it's become a friend. I can imagine the tingle of a limb beginning to fall asleep, the buzz of nerves turning into spikes of pain before finally, finally, there's the welcome numb.

It's worth the ache, in my opinion, to reach that finish line. A reward few can understand.

I'm sure Fred does not have that goal in mind when he says, "I bet I could do it!"

"You think you could?" He couldn't sit still for even half a minute, but I'm a mother who encourages even the boldest of dreams. "Maybe we should paint you up and let you try it?"

"I'll try it now." His trepidation gone, he runs to the empty seat next to the bronze man and attempts to replicate his pose. His little face alternates between imitating the bronze man's seriousness and a pleased smile with himself.

I bite back a laugh, wishing I'd brought my camera. I try not to take it out with us too often on our days together. This time is for him, and it's hard to stay present in that when my mind is consumed with the business of making art.

Right now, though, I want to capture the image for the moment, not the craft. Remembering my mobile, I dig it from my purse and snap a pic on the rarely used camera app, impressed that Freddie has managed to hold the position this long.

"He's a natural," a familiar voice says at my side and like a pleasant breeze on a humid day, I feel a sudden relief.

Trying not to smile too widely, I peer over at Hendrix. "I suppose he is. It's come as a surprise."

Just then, Freddie begins to fidget. Just wrinkling his nose, twice, three times, as though it needs to be itched. "Perhaps I spoke too soon."

Hendrix chuckles, the camera slung across his chest bouncing with the movement. "He seems to really be struggling there. Poor guy."

"You're doing great, Fred! Bravo!"

My encouragement draws a grin on my son's face, wide and toothy. "Told you I could do it!" Then he's up and running toward one of the other living statues. He clearly considers himself their newest coworker and I could watch this all day.

As I follow after him, without discussion, Hendrix does too, matching my stride.

I curse myself for being as thrilled as I am for his company. "Fancy seeing you here," I say when I can't think of anything else and the need to speak to him feels like a butterfly cupped in my hands, its wings beating desperately to escape.

"Yes. Quite a coincidence."

I roll my eyes. At him. At me. No coincidence at all, actually, since the assignment I gave class the day before was to get some shots of the competition today. The statues are perfect models, their stillness removes variables and allows the photographer to focus on other elements—the light, the angle, the story. Also, the performers already expect to be photographed so there isn't the ethics issue of taking pictures without permission, a debate many of my peers have had about snapping pics of people in the park.

"The exhibit goes on all day," I protest. "I could have missed you." It is honestly a stroke of luck that we happen to be here at the same time as he is. I'd tried to be, of course, but I had little hope that it would actually occur.

If I believed in that sort of thing, I might think the universe is trying to tell me something.

"You wouldn't have missed me," he says, and suddenly I know he's been looking for me. That he likely arrived just as the event opened and planned to stay until it closed for just the shot at an encounter.

That patience of his. It unravels me.

Why am I here, why am I here, why am I here? When I told him this isn't what I want. When I insisted to myself that this isn't what I need. Maybe my truest addiction all along was to feeling the happiness he draws out in our talks.

I dragged my child into this tangled mess. How fucked up am I?

Though my selfish reasons for being here seem to be an accidental score because Fred is having a "dynamite" time running from statue to statue, posing next to them. He pretends to raise a gun with the green army men. At the group of golden cowboys, he adopts a tilt to his posture that allows him to fit right in. When he gets to the woman made up to look like a bronze replication of the queen, he bows deeply before her, his small legs teetering in the position.

He's so funny and so fast flitting from one scene to the next that I hardly have time to recover. At one point, I have to bend over to contain the fit of laughter.

When I'm able to stand again, I wipe tears from my eyes and catch Hendrix beaming at me. He's been laughing along with me, and it felt so natural, I forgot that it's not. Forgot that few people ever see me like this, loose and uninhibited.

It makes me feel captured, in a way. I resent him for it, for witnessing this part of me.

But also it makes me want him to see more.

Fred runs back to me, his eyes wild with excitement. "Mummy! Did you see the mermaid?"

I glance around until I spot the woman dressed and painted in green sitting on top of a rock, her mermaid tail dangling down the side. "I see her now. Is she your favorite?"

"So far!" He abruptly settles his elation when he spots Hendrix at my side. "Hello," he says, not the least withdrawn like I am. "I'm Fred. You can call me Freddie."

Hendrix looks to me, and I nod. "What a very adult introduction. Better than what I could have offered myself. I'm Hendrix. You can call me whatever you like, I'll probably answer."

"He talks funny," Fred whispers loudly.

"He does, doesn't he? American dialects are the silliest."

My child beams like we've shared a joke, then addresses Hendrix once again. "Are you Mummy's friend?"

God, the rippling of my insides makes me feel like I'm on the Eye instead of feet flat on the ground. It feels so big, this introduction. A monumental moment between the three of us. And inappropriate since I have no intentions of keeping Hendrix in my life. Irresponsible too. What kind of mixed messages am I giving the man? What kind of mixed message am I giving my son?

But if I were to keep Hendrix…

I don't even know how to fantasize that without an understanding of how he'd fit into my full life when the biggest portion of my life is Fred.

Again the man looks at me. I don't venture an answer, intrigued with what he'll say on his own.

"I'm a student in her class," Hendrix says, a safe answer that I should let stand.

But I'm an idiot of a creature so I amend. "He's in my class, but yes, Fred. Hendrix is a friend."

Hendrix's eyes light and his lips curl up as though he's won a grand prize.

Has he?

No, he hasn't. It's just a fact. We knew each other before he enrolled in my class. He's not just a student.

If we're actually accounting for facts, of course, he's not just a friend, either.

"I don't know many of Mummy's friends," Fred says thoughtfully. "Do you have a kid too?"

It's the natural assumption. Most of the people he has met as "Mummy's friends" were really arranged playdates with mothers who had children Fred's age.

Hendrix squats down so he's eye-to-eye with my son. "I don't. Sort of unfortunate because I always wanted kids."

"Why don't you have one then?"

The questions of children.

It reminds me of the encouragement Hendrix gave the night before, suggesting that it wasn't too late for me to have more. Had I imagined that he was suggesting the possibility of fathering them?

Hendrix shrugs. "Good question. I'll get on that."

Fred nods his head like it's a done deal. "You can pretend I'm your kid for today," he suggests.

Hendrix looks up at me. "I'm not sure how your mother would feel about that."

My chest tightens and releases. Tightens again, and I'm not sure if it's a good feeling or a bad one. Not sure if it's okay to let my child play out this whim or if it'll do long-term damage.

But oh, what a delicious whim it is. A fantasy I'll play over and over, having a partner in loving my son. Someone to share the wonder and joy of watching this little miracle discover the world. A partner who loves me just as devotedly. Who wants to discover the world with me.

I don't have to respond, thankfully, because Fred shrugs it off like it's no big deal, and then is instantly distracted by a wizard statue in the distance.

"Stay within sight," I shout as he runs off ahead of us.

"I'm sorry about that," Hendrix says. "I hope it didn't make you too uncomfortable."

I shake my head, trying to adopt the same nonchalance as Fred. "Not your fault. He's just starting to realize he doesn't have a dad, and I think it fascinates him that there are men who might want to be one." I barely let a beat go by before adding, "And don't ask about his father, please. He passed away before Fred was born, and that's all I like to say about that."

"Understood." He's quiet now as we walk. I've ruined the mood. Which is probably for the best since I'm not trying to form any attachments between us.

Any more attachments between us.

Still, I can't help being sour over it. I'm so busy brooding, in fact, that it's Hendrix who has to point it out. "Look," he says. His face says that he's charmed by something. I know that because I've seen him look at me in the same way.

I follow his gaze and see Freddie standing in front of the gray-stone colored wizard, his expression full of wonder.

Quickly and with stealth, Hendrix approaches them, taking the lens off his camera and bringing it to his eye as he does. I creep behind him with equal excitement, hoping he caught the picture I'm seeing in my own head.

"Let me see," I say eagerly when he pauses his clicking to look at the screen. He hands over the camera willingly.

The photos are good. They're really good. Much better than the shots he took in class yesterday. These aren't missing what those lacked.

Still.

"May I?"

He understands me immediately, taking the sling off his shoulder so I can use the camera. Slowly, hoping that Freddie stays exactly as he is, I crouch down and manually adjust the focus. I only click three times, but when I stand up again, I have exactly the shot I envisioned—Freddie looking up at the wizard with awe, taken from his height so that the wizard appears as looming to the observer as he does to the child.

"That's it," Hendrix says as he peers over my shoulder. "That's the shot."

It's twenty-two degrees, and I'm warm under my long-sleeve floral wrap dress, but I shiver at his words. Just like I've never had a partner parent, I've never had a partner in my other aspects of creation.

I hadn't ever imagined how much I might want them.

"Look at the witch!" Freddie is off again, running toward a bronze woman with snakes for hair.

"She's Medusa," I correct, handing back the camera to its owner. I start in the direction Freddie headed, then stop with a frown.

Hendrix stops with me, slinging the camera over his shoulder. "What's—?" He catches sight of what caught my eye, or rather *who* caught my eye. "I didn't come with her," he says, seeming to know how much I want to hear it.

He probably didn't. Kaila with an i had the same assignment that Hendrix did. Of course there was every chance she'd be here, too.

I force a smile and wave at my other student, grateful that she's too consumed with her photography to do anything more than wave back.

It doesn't do anything to lighten the lead in my stomach.

Hendrix is deeply in tune with my displeasure. "It's the first time I've seen her all day. Swear."

It shouldn't matter. It *doesn't*. He can do what he pleases. He has no need to give me excuses.

Yes, my jealousy is irrational, but it's as real and spectacular as the humans pretending to be stone. "Why would I think otherwise?" I say cattily. "Because she's here at the exact same time you are. Because she partnered up with you in class. Because you bought her a negroni while she hung on you at Nightsky."

It's amazing how Hendrix tolerates my petty behavior. "She said to get whatever I was getting," he says simply. "And she was the one doing all the hanging."

"You went with her to the bar in the first place. She arranged it, I'm guessing?"

"She did," he admits. "Remember there was a group of us."

"But she's the one who asked you."

He steps closer to me, his body almost brushing against my arms crossed over my chest, and though I'm acutely aware what we might look like to Kaila, to any other student observing us, I don't move away. "And I said yes," he says quietly, "because I was already planning to go as soon as you told the class you liked to go there too."

I glance up at him, needing to hear what I so shouldn't hear. "Why?"

"Because I wanted to see you. And so I went to where I thought it was most likely that would happen."

The photographer-in-wait. Staking out the subject's known habitat.

"Some women file restraining orders over such behavior." I say it like a dare, though I don't know what I'm daring him to do.

"Tell me to stop, and I'll stop."

Was that what I wanted him to say? Because how easy. It's one simple word that will magically put all this to an end.

But I can't make the word form on my lips. I can't even think it in my mind. Because as much as I say I don't want this, as much as I pretend I don't want him, we both know it's a lie.

So if not stop, what now? Do we follow each other around? Do we continue to do this, whatever this is, every time we "bump into each other"?

How long is he going to stay interested in that?

But more importantly, what happens to my happiness if I don't let him in?

I drop my arms and step away, needing space, but I only end up angling one side of my body from him because I can't bear to be any farther away. "Why do you care? Was it the sex?"

"No." He looks disgusted that I even asked. "Don't get me wrong. It was fucking amazing sex. Mind-blowing sex. Out-of-this world sex. Both times. I've honestly never felt more at home than I did inside you, Camilla. But do not ever think to degrade this to just sex." He waggles a finger from him to me on the word "this," indicating the crazy attraction that exists between us.

He feels it too.

It makes me want to cry, and I'm not certain if they'd be happy tears or sad. Sometimes they feel the same. Bubbles. "You shouldn't say such things to me, Hendrix. I left last night when you started talking like this, remember."

He lets his hand brush against mine purposefully. His pinkie strokes up and down mine, letting me know how purposeful the move is. "The only thing I regret last night is not kissing you."

My breathing becomes heavy. I thought about that too, all night as I lay in the dark. I repeated the entire dinner over and over, the kiss we didn't have ending each replay.

I almost say it too.

But that's too honest. Too naked.

I pretend he didn't say it and double down on my previous statement. "You should find another tactic. The heart-on-your-sleeve method isn't working."

"I don't know. It seems my tactic is working just fine."

"Really?"

He wraps his pinkie around mine and electricity shoots up my arm like the light going on when the plug is locked in place. "You're here, aren't you?"

I blink up at him, then have to immediately lower my gaze because it's too hard to look at him and feel all the things I feel at the same time. "I don't know what I'm doing," I say, my voice trembling with the confession.

"I know," he says, and it isn't at all patronizing. "We'll go slow. We'll figure it out together."

I can't speak except to say, "I have to go."

And when I get Freddie and head us in the direction of Edward's for our swim, I haven't the least idea if I'm walking away or toward.

Chapter Eight

Tension: The state of being stretched or strained. - *MoMA Glossary of Art Terms*

Three minutes until class, and I'm as nervous as I was on day one.

This time, instead of worrying that the Hendrix Reid listed on my class sheet is the same one that I met in the autumn, I'm flustered because I'm sure that it is.

Excited too.

There's a quote that comes to mind from a famous musical when Little Red Riding Hood has first met the wolf, the fear she has at seeing his teeth bared is equally balanced with excitement.

I feel that way about Hendrix, not that I believe he's a wolf per se. But he *could* be. He could be any kind of man. He could be secretly cruel. He could lash out when he drinks too much. He could use his fists when he doesn't get his way.

Or he could be the gentlest man on the face of the planet.

That last possibility might actually scare me the most. I've found the other sorts of men so typical in my life that I feel unfortunately experienced. I'm not sure what to do with kindness. Not sure how to take love that doesn't feel like a wound except from Edward and Freddie.

It's a wonder that the past six days away from him hasn't given me time to rethink and reform. Going to the park, letting him meet my son—those were risks I should never have taken. And though I left that day with a light step and an uncharacteristically pleasant outlook, I had fully expected it wouldn't last long outside his presence.

But strangely, it has. The time in between made room for doubts, yes, but it also allowed hope to settle. Allowed excitement to burrow into me. By mid-week, my yearning was stronger than my fear, and all I could think about was being close to him again, no matter what the cost.

God, why does he make me wait? Is he not as anxious to see me again too? Has he changed his mind? What if he's given up and doesn't show at all? Each second that passes, the room feels darker and smaller, too dark and small to hold the growing mass of anticipation within me. My heart is pounding. I'm practically in a sweat. I'm about to spin from the winding tension.

It *is* an addiction.

Then, thirty seconds to start time, as my hope leans toward turmoil, he walks in the door, bringing a beam of sunlight with him and a stream of fresh air.

Our eyes meet instantly. His lips twitch. His gaze is warm. He's so obviously happy to see me that even I can't find a way to twist the proof into something other than what it is.

I have to clamp down the kind of grin I want to give him. I present a smile more suitable for the entire class instead and launch into the day's lesson. "Studio portraits. Where light is your best friend and your worst foe. Let's take it on, shall we?"

The half hour spent on lecture goes well enough, despite the split in my attention. I have to force myself not to rush. Each word spoken brings me closer to the breakout sessions when the students will be let loose to work, and I'll walk around to counsel them.

This time, I will not leave Hendrix for the end.

It's still another thirty minutes after I'm done teaching that I actually get to him. Working in the studio is a foreign experience for many of them and much help is needed setting up backdrops and softbox and umbrella lights before the first shoot can begin. Eventually, though, there's a student on a stool and another with her camera focused on her. The others are lined up to take a turn as photographer, and I'm free.

I somehow manage not to run straight to him, stopping to go over the weekend's assignment with Charlie and then Salima before I wander over to Hendrix. The anticipation is delicious, even the smallest buildup of time echoing vastly inside me.

"May I?" I say, reaching for his camera. Our fingers brush as I take it, and it's not an accident.

I bend my head over the screen, slowly flipping through images that barely register as they pass by. I'm focused on the perception I'm giving to the others who might be watching rather than his work. I'm focused on how near he's standing. On the rise and fall of his breaths. On the sprout of happiness inside that's grown from the seed he planted.

"I can't stop thinking about you." My words are quiet, and we're nestled near a corner in the back, but I glance around the room casually just in case.

"You don't know how happy I am to hear that." His voice isn't quite as low, probably not necessary since what he's said is more innocuous. He could be happy that I like his composition. He could be happy that I think the sun will stay out all day. He could be happy that I liked the sushi bar he recommended.

It's a little bit of a game, I realize, pretending in front of the others. A thrilling bit of taboo.

I look up at him, eager to connect with his gaze. "You had me wrecked when you didn't show up until the last minute for class. Kept me on pins and needles waiting for you."

I'm surprised I'm being so forthright. It's almost as if I have no choice. The feelings have been so bottled up inside me, they spill out like a shaken-up fizzy pop once the top comes off.

He rewards my honesty with a smirk. "Now you know how I feel."

My ribs tighten and the smile flickers on my lips as I try to decide if I'm bothered by being called out. Trying to decide if I'm supposed to feel guilty.

"I'm used to that feeling from waiting in the field," he says, reading my apprehension correctly, and this time his voice is nearly a whisper. "I'm comfortable with feeling it. No pressure, Camilla. I'm okay."

I nod, air moving through my lungs as my chest loosens. "Was your motive payback then?" I ask playfully.

"Nope. I'm just very bad with time." He pauses for my chuckle. As though he expected one. As though I give them easily. Only with him. "To be honest, I got here much too early, so early the door wasn't unlocked yet. Then, when I saw you approaching, I suddenly worried I was being too presumptuous or too, I don't know. Eager. So I slipped off to take some pics for a while. Got caught up in that and forgot to watch when to come back."

I've been there. Many a time. The inner world of the artist is awfully large. It's easy to get lost in it.

But that's not the part of what he's said that requires commentary. "You came early?"

He nods, a shy grin forming. "I couldn't wait to see you."

"I couldn't wait to see you either."

I'm not sure if the words feel better in or out at first, but after they hang for a few seconds, crackling the air around us, I decide I like them there. I like him knowing. I want to share that happy sprout with him instead of keeping it hidden.

A shuffle in the background as the student posing switches off with one in line draws my attention back to our surroundings. My skin feels itchy all of a sudden. "You're a student," I say, forcing my eyes back to his camera. "I keep wondering if this is inappropriate."

"Do I need to point out that nothing inappropriate has happened?"

"The kinds of thoughts I keep having feel very different." There I am again being candid.

"Well." He moves a step closer, and the closure of the distance between us combined with the throatiness of that single syllable has my thighs clenching. "Considering that all of your students are adults and that this isn't the type of school where you give a grade or wield power in another way over us, I think you could probably fuck each and every one of them and no one would bat an eye."

"Fuck the lot of them then?" My cheeks feel warm, and I'm very near giggling. I hardly recognize who I am with him.

He's abruptly serious when he answers. "Please don't do that."

"Not any of them?"

"Maybe just one."

I'm so risk aversive that I'd all but forgotten the sweet misery in being dangerous, in saying dangerous things.

And these are dangerous words. Because there's still a bit of the forbidden, no matter what he says, but mostly because there's an underlying challenge to this exchange. An admission that we've been thinking about each other in the naughtiest of ways. An invitation to make those naughty ways come to life.

I want him. I do. I've never stopped wanting him.

But the suggestion reminds me of the last time, of how I moved naked against him in the dark. Pursuing this with him will mean more of the same, good and bad. What are the chances that his flat has blackout curtains as well?

Instinctively, I tug at the cuff of my sleeve while my stomach ties itself in knots. "There might not be grades given, but there was money put forth. I should at least appear to be giving you all equal attention."

With that, I turn my head back to the camera screen and try to nudge my focus to the images before me and away from the gnawing tension in my gut. It's impossible, of course. How did I end up here, standing on the edge of this precipice? I've been so drawn by the view that I forgot how sharp the cliff was.

The photos pass in a blur as I scroll through. Vaguely I'm aware of the scenery changing, of the series moving from the living statues competition to another familiar setting—the walkway outside the school. I freeze on the image of someone that I know entirely too well, one that I have argued with and gone to war with. One I have tried to reason with, tried to love, tried to hate just as much.

It's exquisitely composed. The proportion is spot on, my body filling exactly as much of the image as it should to be compelling. The angle is remarkable and unique, the lighting superb the way it hits my face as I lift my chin to the sky. The story is quite clear—a woman who has found the sun before it disappears behind the clouds. I would see it perfectly even if I wasn't the subject, even if I hadn't lived it.

Seeing myself on his screen like this, in this context, a shot taken without my knowledge, without even knowing I was being watched—it makes me feel all sorts of twisted, like I'm tangled up in barbed wire. He had no right to take this without my permission. He has no right to see me this clearly. He has no right to make me feel this exposed.

He had no right to take the first image of that other me. She should have been mine.

The emotions would be best stored and sorted through later, but my words seem to always come out untethered around Hendrix. "How dare you?" I ask, not careful about my volume. "You were watching me when I arrived? How dare you?"

He gapes, shocked by my outburst.

He's not the only one watching. I feel the eyes of all my students on me like needles, and I still can't pin my mouth shut. "You can't just take pictures of people without their consent. It's unethical. It's wrong. It's not fucking nice."

I'm shaking with anger and something else. Something I'm so unused to I have trouble naming it. Vulnerability? It makes me feel stripped down and smothered all at once, and I *know*. I know the feeling only partly stems from the stolen photograph, that I'm being ridiculous, and that the bulk of my ire is rooted in this cyclone of a situation that I'm in with Hendrix. It's defense against the possibility that this happiness is false. I've moved from the calm of the eye into the overwhelming winds of the storm, but that knowledge does nothing to leash my temper.

"Camilla," Hendrix says, naturally taken aback. "I didn't know. I'm sorry."

Tears sting at my eyes, and I can't look at him. Turning away means facing everyone else—twelve faces wearing identical shocked expressions.

"That goes for all of you. No photos without consent. Ever. Not in my classroom. I won't accept it." It's not a believable cover. It's not enforceable. It's not even practical.

I can't deal with those details at the moment. I'm dizzy and unsettled and embarrassed and there's no way I can stay here like this, bare and on display.

"Take this." Without looking at him, I hand Hendrix his camera. "Continue on, please," I say to everyone else.

Then, heading to the door with even steps, I run.

Chapter Nine

Expression: The means by which an artist communicates ideas and emotions. - *MoMA Glossary of Art Terms*

I was sixteen the first time I picked up a camera. One of those early therapists Edward hired had suggested it. It wasn't the first activity I'd been prescribed. The Four Ps, that doctor had called his recommendations—painting, piano, poetry, and photography. Four Ps for therapy. I'd been an utter failure with the first three, so I was less than thrilled when he'd informed my brother it was time to try the last.

"Less than thrilled" is a kind way of describing how I'd felt, actually. I broke the first camera I'd been given—a Kodak DCS that had cost over ten thousand. Digital was still new and this one was cutting edge, which was why Edward had selected it. Inaccurate as the feeling may have been, I had a sense that the gift had been an attempt to buy my forgiveness for the time after foster care that I'd been enrolled in private school. It was no secret that I harbored resentment. I made it known whenever possible, including when I'd opened that box, seen the expensive contraption, and proceeded to throw it across the room.

I have a different view of that time now that I'm an adult. It was hard enough to become a parent in my thirties. I can't imagine what it must have been like to have to parent a sister at the age of eighteen, especially a sister with as much baggage as I'd had. Have. Some of that baggage I share with Edward. Our well-to-do household fell apart when our mother died. My father, distraught by her loss, chose her over us and ended his life to be with her in the grave. Thanks to a swindling relative, the fortune he'd left us was soon gone, and both Edward and I ended up being separated in the foster care system until he was old enough to assume guardianship over me. Luckily, he'd inherited our father's ambition and quickly built his own wealth, which is helpful but didn't fix anything. All the money in the world couldn't erase the damage done. As a teen, I made sure I let him know it often.

Edward did the best that he could, I know. I did the best that I could too, and, unfortunately, while he had his own issues to work through, he fared much better than I did.

It's part of the reason I've kept that secret hope of a sibling for Freddie in my heart. It would be another chance at the relationship Edward and I were robbed of when our parents died.

Thankfully, Edward was always a patient man, particularly when it comes to what he believes in, and he believed in me. Yes, he admonished me for the outburst, but he also bought me another, this time allowing me to choose the camera for myself.

Instead of going for a fancy digital model, I selected a Nikon 35mm. I was drawn to the process of developing film. Truly, that was the only thing that excited me about the idea of photography—the hours I'd get to spend tucked away in the dark.

It was quite a surprise when I discovered the real joy was behind the camera, with one eye pressed to the viewfinder, the other closed tightly so that my whole world narrowed into what was in front of me. And that world was completely shaped by me. No one else.

It was life-changing. I was able to take the emotions I had bottled up inside and place them outside of myself. I could look at them from a different angle. I could detach.

I'm not sure if it achieved the goal that my therapist had intended since I soon moved on to another. But even through the long string of specialists that followed, I clung to my photography. It was an art that became a fast friend. An only friend sometimes. In the darkest days with Frank, taking pictures was most often my only form of escape. No matter how much he bruised and mangled my body, he had no power over what I chose to express. He didn't get to be the author of the stories I told.

I learned to tell those stories in other ways over the years, more destructive ways. Sex has become another favorite method of expression as long as I am the initiator, because though it involves a participant, I get to choose it. After all the men in my life that chose what happened to my body for me, fucking at my whim is a powerful reminder that I'm the one who has control now.

It's a false reminder, though. I might be able to direct how and when and what happens physically during the act, but I still can't control the things that happen inside me. It's the same across all forms of expression, whether it be with my pussy or my camera or a knife, I can only control the external, and not even much of that.

The reality is I am still powerless.

I am still subject to my emotions.

I am still shaped by the actions of people outside of me.

I am still very much human.

* * * *

It only takes a quick trip to the restroom to pull myself together. I'm still flushed with humiliation when I walk in the door, partly because I didn't take my key and had to knock to be let in, but it's not so bad I can't show my face.

Dr. Joseph would count that as growth.

I'm more reluctant to name it so until I discover what I do in the future. The important reactions aren't always immediate, I've found, but rather what happens later, usually in the dark, when I'm alone and free to really express myself.

For now, I'm composed enough to be attentive to the students, mentoring them through the rest of the day's activity.

Not all the students, of course. I stay clear of Hendrix, unable or unwilling to even glance at him. I'm not sure if I'm too angry or too embarrassed or if I'm simply too scared to see how he might look at me now. To see if the reflection of me he wears in his expression has changed.

It's a tension that I carry throughout the rest of the class, as I count down the time remaining before this exhausting session is through. Half an hour. A quarter of an hour. Ten minutes. Now five.

Finally, I give this week's assignment and dismiss them.

I turn my back to them immediately, not watching as they leave. There is much to clean up today since we worked in the studio. Lights that need to be unplugged, backdrops that need to be rolled and stowed. I'll get to all of it soon enough. Right now all I can do is lean my palms on one of the work tables and try not to think. Try to breathe. Try not to wonder if Hendrix will be there when I turn around.

I tell myself that if he is or if he isn't, that will be my answer.

Not entirely sure what the question is. Maybe having the answer will help me figure it out.

I wait until I hear the door click. It's shut now. If he's on the other side of the door, he's not coming back without me letting him in. I slowly count to ten. The room is silent. Too quiet for company. I'm certain I'm alone by the time I'm brave enough to pivot.

I'm relieved to find my "certainty" is flawed. He's here, hands shoved in his pockets, camera bag hanging from his shoulders.

And God, his eyes. The way they look at me. What he sees hasn't changed at all.

"Camilla…" I can't blame him for not knowing what to say. He tries again. "I didn't mean to—"

I don't give him a chance to finish before I'm advancing across the room, my palms itching until they're wrapped in his collar, jerking his face toward mine.

His mouth is tentative against mine at first. Questioning. No man has ever shown me I'm the one with the power like this before. It's intoxicating, even though we're almost barely doing this. He tries to pull away once, but it's a halfhearted attempt, and when he gives in, he gives in entirely. His lips part, inviting in my tongue. He drops his bag on the floor—gently enough to do no damage, but not nearly as gentle as I'm sure he normally handles his camera—and his arms wrap around my waist. I'm tugged flush to him so I feel the whole of him against me. I feel his heat merge with mine. Feel the hardening bulge at my abdomen.

I've never kissed someone so urgently. Never clawed at a man's trousers like they hid my only source of survival. Never got out of my own pants so quickly that I tripped during their removal.

And I've been frantic to fuck before. Hendrix and I were frenzied that first time in France, but this feeling is even more fraught. There's an added desperation that I can't quite name. I'm not secretly praying that he'll know what he's doing or for a decent-sized cock like I was back then. I already know that he does and that makes these seconds of anticipation all the more intense.

He's just as manic as I, fumbling for a condom, tossing his wallet behind him before ripping the package open with his teeth. I'm more hindrance when I attempt to help him roll it on, but I can't help myself. I need to touch his cock. I need to be part of the action required to get him inside of me.

Finally it's on, and with a grunt, Hendrix hoists me up. I hook my ankles around his waist while he notches his cock at my entrance. It proves difficult in this position, and instead of trying to work it out where we stand, the man is smart enough to carry me to the worktable. My bare ass meets the wood, and with my legs still around him, the angle is just right for him to push inside.

I cry out on the first thrust. It's always a delicious sort of torment, as my body stretches to accommodate girth, as the empty place inside me is filled. There's an added satisfaction of discovering that the memories of my night with Hendrix were not a trick of the mind. We really do fit perfectly. The happy hum, under everything. He really does make me momentarily feel whole.

I'm tempted to make him slow down so I can draw out the ecstasy, though I'm unsure either of us could hold back right now. The tempo seems to be driving us rather than the other way around, as though the force that compels us toward each other is in charge here. As though our fucking has been orchestrated by a higher power.

It's nearly unbearable being this out-of-control.

And it's euphoric all at the same time.

I cling to him, not just with my legs, but my arms too, wrapped tight around his neck, holding on to him like an anchor. When that's not enough, I press my forehead against his. Together we peer down between us where his cock disappears repeatedly inside my pussy, and without looking at his eyes, I'm sure he's as mesmerized by the erotic sight.

It looks like being chased, the way his cock returns again and again to nest inside me. I'm wrecked with pleasure and absent of much coherent thought, but I wonder fleetingly if being caught by him for real would feel as good as it does when he's buried to the hilt.

It's so terrifyingly thrilling of an idea that it sends me into orgasm, and the thought is lost in the whirlwind of bliss that spins me, unwrapping me until every good thing inside is unleashed at once. I'm dizzy from the ecstasy, limp and spent and dazed.

His release follows right after, his accompanying moan ragged and relieved, as though he'd been waiting for me and the wait had been hard. The head start to recovery should be to my benefit, but I'm still having trouble with my breath when he grips my chin and places his mouth over my own.

Has kissing always been this monumental? Was there always so much communicated between lips and tongues moving together like ours are now?

I'm not sure I have the strength for what's being said.

I break away first, letting it happen in stages. A slowing of my tongue. The closing of my lips. The arching away of my spine.

He's not ready to let me go. I can tell with the way he pulls me back to place a kiss on my cheek, then on my eyebrow. Now on my hair.

I set my hands on my thighs and note the contrast of the bare skin against my sleeve-covered arms. It's as much as I can give. I cannot give any more.

"I shouldn't have assumed," he says, his cheek pressed against my forehead. "I know you aren't at all like the creatures I shoot in the field, but I'm not used to considering consent."

I shake my head against him. I gave consent, albeit silently. For my body. It's my heart I'm protecting now. "You did nothing wrong. It's me."

It's always me.

I nudge him away and jump down from the table. I keep my back to him until I'm put back together, which goes smoother than the undressing. When I've turned around again, the condom's been taken care of, and his cock's put away, and now it's time to put us away as well.

"This is the end of this," I tell him. "It's out of our system, and it can't happen again."

I think I hope that he'll leave now. Or maybe I hope that he'll stay, which he does.

"Why?" he asks, and it's not like he's angry, he just wants to know.

What a complicated question, though. With complicated answers.

Or perhaps they're really simple.

"I'm your teacher," I say, which is the truth and also a lie.

"That's not why. What's the real why?"

"It's as much why as I need to give you." I fold my arms over my chest, like I'm closing a door.

He studies me for long seconds. "When the class is over, what then?"

Fuck, I didn't bloody think this through.

And now I'm worried I might cry.

"Is it really what you want, Camilla? For this to never happen again?"

I swallow hard. *Yes*, I mean to say. Instead what comes out is, "No."

Before he can take that admission and run with it, I say more. "But also yes. It's what I need. And that's more important than what I want right now."

He studies me some more. He considers. He swears under his breath. "I shouldn't have let this happen. I knew that sex needed to stay out of this because you would find a way to make that an ending. I knew this was a bad idea."

He's right, and yet I'm hurt. "It's my fault then. If you were so all-knowing, why didn't you try harder to push me away?"

"Because I fucking want you, Camilla." It's the sharpest he's ever been with me, and it's still softer than Frank ever was. How can I let this in, knowing there's any possibility of it ending? "Because I want your skin and your mouth and your brain. And your pain."

The last word closes me up tighter. "I don't know what you're inferring. I'm fine."

Isn't that what people say when they're exactly the opposite of fine?

He takes a step toward me. "You can tell me. I'll listen. I'm not going to judge."

I'm trembling with rage. Or fear. It's all muddled up. All I know is that he needs to stop. "You don't know what you're talking about."

I turn toward the equipment that needs to be put away, an excuse to be done with this conversation.

"I felt you, Camilla," he says to my back. "I felt your body that night. I felt your skin."

A bolt of terror strikes like lightning through me. "Don't."

"Did someone do it to you?" He pauses. "Or did you do it to yourself?"

Pins and needles spike every inch of my skin. I whirl around to face him. "You need to leave."

"Camilla…"

"Leave! Now!"

He knows he's crossed the line. He's been around enough wild animals to know when they've turned dangerous.

He picks up his camera bag on his way out and opens the door before he pauses with a sigh. His head turns toward me. "Leave forever? Or just leave for today?"

Forever.
Or not at all.
The bubble floats between us.
What answer should I give?
I give him the truth. "I don't know."

Chapter Ten

Background: The area of an artwork that appears farthest away from the viewer; also, the area against which a figure or scene is placed. - *MoMA Glossary of Art Terms*

After class, I'm too distracted to spend my free day as I usually do. There's a new exhibit at The Gallery and a farmer's market I'd meant to visit.

I come home, instead. With Sylvia here to nanny, I can tuck myself away in my room, pull the covers over my head and sleep through the rest of the day if I want to. I do want to.

But my mind's too buzzy for sleep.

I find myself lying on the floor in the playroom with Freddie while Sylvia fixes him lunch. Silly if I thought this would help. It's often a difficult task to be completely in the moment with a six-year-old, especially when there are pressing items to give attention to. The work to do sitting in my inbox. The discrepancy in the electric bill that needs to be sorted. The manicure that's well past due. The opportunities that could be taken with my camera and the late afternoon light.

Typically, I can lose myself in the simple pleasures of watching my son. He'll never know the childhood I had. His occasional loneliness will never touch how alone I felt. Typically, knowing that is enough to make me happy enough too.

This is not a typical day.

Luckily, he seems preoccupied with his latest Lego creation. The kid is truly an artist, absurdist with his concepts, perhaps, but he definitely has a point of view.

I should tell him as much. I should extol his work and encourage his thirst for experimentation, but I'm feeling self-centered and self-loathing and all I can do is stare at the ceiling and think, *not enough not enough not enough.*

It's like a woodpecker tapping at my brain. Incessant and maddening. My groan of frustration comes involuntarily like a yawn, starting small and growing as it takes over.

"Mummy?" Fred's concern is etched in his brows as he peers over at me, his sticky fingers clutching a Lego in midair.

I might appreciate this aspect of motherhood the most. It's impossible to truly lose myself in self-pity with my child there to remind me the world does not revolve around my heartache. That for one soul, I am enough. Even when I feel the opposite.

"Sorry," I say, rolling to my side and propping my head up with my forearm. "I'm fine."

He's not convinced. "Did you hurt yourself?"

I shake my head, but I remember my commitment to parenting with transparency. There is something Fred might learn here, even if it's just that adults are not immune to complicated feelings.

I think about the simplest way to frame my current emotional state, a way he'll understand. "I'm obsessing," I tell him eventually. "I can't stop thinking about something I want very badly. It's making me feel a little insane."

His face relaxes. He can understand that. There is more than one tantrum that has occurred because of something he had to have Right This Minute. But there's still a question in his expression. "You're a grown-up. Can't you just get the thing you want?"

I open my mouth and shut it again, replaying his words in my head. *Yes, Camilla, can't you just get the thing you want? Who told you that you weren't allowed to be happy? The only one who ever did is gone now. Can't you get it for yourself now?*

Out of the mouths of babes.

* * * *

It's easier said than done, of course. But once the decision is made, it does seem less hard than I imagined to choose what to wear, to know where to go, to not worry about what I'll say. I simply remember the feeling and chase the effervescent trail it's left between me and the man who showed me how to find it.

It still takes a while to get ready. I primp in every manner of the word. It's been ages since I've taken this much care in my appearance, painting my toenails, plucking my brows, shaving every last blade of unwanted hair.

It isn't until I'm standing outside Nightsky that I have my first flutter of uncertainty, and it's not doubt about what I have planned, but that there's a possibility I won't get the opportunity to carry it out. It doesn't scare me as much as it should, because I'm finally starting to recognize that as much as I find my happiness in him, it's because that spark inside me has been lit. It's not a stranger to me anymore, this feeling. I might, someday, be able to chance this sprout growing into a vine of my own. But first, I want to see if this man who adored my child and looks at me like art would like to keep watering it with me.

I definitely won't have the chance standing out here, so with a prayer uttered under my breath, I push through the door and sweep my eyes across the room.

My gaze finds Hendrix almost instantly, even though his back is to me as he sits at the bar.

I allow the sigh of relief before heading toward him. He still hasn't looked behind him when I take the empty seat at his side. I feel how he notices me, how his back straightens and the air crackles like his body has just been turned on.

I also feel his hesitation, the worry that he might be overstepping by being here.

"Should I make it two?" he asks, picking up his near empty glass. He still hasn't turned toward me.

"No, thank you. I didn't come here tonight to drink."

Now he swivels in my direction so we're face-to-face. "Then why did you come here?"

"I wanted to see you. And so I came to where I thought it was most likely that would happen." I've quoted him, and it hits the mark.

He smiles, slowly but surely. He looks lonely, somehow, under that confidence.

My smile matches his without even trying. We're caught like that for several seconds, taking each other in, saying nothing. Something hits me

like a ton of bricks. The me he's seen that I wasn't sure was really me…
Could it be that what he saw was us all along? Entwined, making each
other better? Finding happy, discovering a new world?

Eventually, I realize I'm the one driving here, and so, gently, I put my
foot on the gas. "Could we go somewhere?" I don't want him to assume
I'm up to my old tricks, simply trying to get him in bed, so I add, "To
talk?"

I'd offer my flat but I can't keep towing Freddie into my adult affairs,
and besides, this discussion would be much more appropriate in a kid-free
zone.

He considers for only a moment, though it's long enough to have my
stomach in knots. "I'm subletting an apartment just a couple of blocks
over. If you don't mind small…"

"Just so long as it's private."

"It's definitely that."

A few minutes later, we're outside and now my stomach's knots can
be blamed on what I'm soon to share. I have my talking points
memorized. They're only daunting because they're words I've never said
outside a therapist's office. While they're always trapped inside me, they
feel heavier as we venture from the commercial area of the neighborhood
into the residential. I remind myself that bravery isn't a lack of fear. I
remind myself that a loss leaves me the same, whereas the rewards leave
me infinitely richer.

Then his hand finds mine swinging at my side, his fingers lace
through mine and suddenly the burden lightens, like he's carrying it with
me, and I'm no longer alone.

Romantic notion, I'm aware. It surprises me to find I'm capable of
those.

By the time we're inside his flat and the door is shut behind us, it
feels like we've had an entire conversation though we've spoken very few
words at all. There's much that is said with hands clasped in silence. I
gather a lot was said just by my showing up at all.

But now it's time to transition from that beat to the next, and I'm not
as brazen as I was just a few minutes ago. I wipe my sweaty palms against
the fabric of my skirt as I spin slowly, taking in his space. It's an open
concept, which suits him, and though I'm sure the furniture came with the
rental, there are pieces of him evident everywhere my eyes land. A jacket
thrown over the back of the armchair. A tripod set up by the window.

The photo printer sitting on the kitchen table.

It's been so long since I've been in a place where someone else lived, as temporary as that living arrangement might be. I've forgotten how to settle in.

"Can I get you something?" Hendrix asks, and I sense he's trying to help with my unease.

"Some water maybe?"

"Bottled or in a glass?"

"Either is fine."

He's back too soon, handing me a cold plastic bottle before gesturing at the couch. I take a swallow of the drink and sit down, but as soon as he sits down beside me, I pop back up.

"No, stay there, please," I say when he seems about to follow. I recap the water and set it on the side table, then reach for the tie on my wrap-dress. I have to do this now. Bravery always seems to cower in the face of comfort.

I can feel a protest pushing at his lips, but before he can voice it, I turn my back toward him and lower my dress so that my shoulder blades are exposed, pulling my hair to one side to be sure the scars aren't covered.

The sight renders him speechless. I get it. Sometimes when I catch a glimpse of myself in the three-sided mirror in my closet, I'm rendered speechless too.

I twist my head to glance at Hendrix. "Cigarette burns," I say, in case he can't identify the source of the constellation of angry red marks across my upper back. "My foster father's favorite form of punishment. Punishment being an excuse, really, since I rarely caused trouble back then. Making me wrack my brain trying to figure out what I'd done was part of his sadistic game, I think."

"Camilla..." he says, as he so often does, and I'm desperate to hear what he'll say next, but more eager to plow through the rest.

So I lower my dress farther, until the material is bowed down to my waist and the dark jagged stripe across my mid-back is exposed. "This one was Frank's doing. My husband. We'd been on a walk, and I smiled too wide at a man riding by on his bicycle so as soon as he was out of sight, I was pushed into the barbed wire fence at the side of the road. Later, he claimed it was an accident, but even if he hadn't held me down when he'd pushed...Well, let's just say there was a pattern of such accidents.

"There's matching streaks on the back of my thighs too, and here." I gather my hair high in a fist. "Very slightly you can see the one on the back of my neck."

Hendrix cranes forward so I perch myself on the ottoman in front of him so he can see better. His fingers whisper across the scars, skin that hasn't been touched in years. Certainly it's never been touched this gently.

"It seems stupid, probably, that a woman who was abused as a child would marry someone who treated her the same. Would stay with him." I swallow back against the shame. Even when I think I've overcome it, when I can stand to look at my reflection for days at a time, the feeling returns when I'm being observed. Shame is a weed. It always comes back. "Apparently it's not uncommon. So stupid, but not alone."

"I didn't say you were stupid." His tone is reverent. His tone is awed.

His tone is not full of pity, and that gives me strength to go on. "I have more, not all of them are as easy to see, and I don't remember where half of them came from, what injury left what mark." The breath I take in is shuddering. *Bravery is facing fear.*

On the exhale, I pull my arms out of the sleeves, letting my dress fall off completely as I pivot toward him. "It's these, though, that are the most humiliating."

He takes my outstretched forearm and gazes down at the short lines, stacked evenly on top of each other like rungs of a ladder or like the marks on the wall in Edward's nursery where Freddie stands once a month to measure his height.

Hendrix traces his finger across one. Now the next one. And the next. At the beginning of each stroke, I try to gather the courage to say the rest. At the end of each stroke, I fail.

"You did these," he says for me.

I nod, the ball too big in my throat for words. A deep breath, and it breaks up some. "I was at private school by then. Edward had sent me after he was granted guardianship. Someone had left a boxcutter in the common room."

I hadn't made them all at once. They'd come little by little over a term, each individual cut slashed into my skin when the complexity of emotion inside me became overbearing. It was that fizzy pop again, the way adrenaline poured out of me with the swipe of the knife. Like a release valve for my feelings. Unlike unwanted emotion, a wound had a start and an end, a finite amount of hurt. It was therapeutic. It was art.

But I've tried to explain the poetry of my actions before and been frowned at disapprovingly, so I don't try now. I know it was unhealthy. I know how it would break me to see Fred do it. I also know it was the only way I ever knew to process my pain, from the first burn on. A prescribed timeline. The promise of the end of the suffering. "Don't ask why," I say simply. "It's not something I can put into words."

"You don't have to," he assures me. "They tell a story all on their own."

I twist so I'm facing him directly, and though it's been a long time since I've sat in only my bra and pants in front of a man, the marks on my forearm are the only part of my skin that feel exposed. "What story do they tell?" I ask, because I'm honestly curious.

While I wait for his answer, I feel the same anxious anticipation that builds when waiting for a critic to explain what meaning they picked up from my latest photography exhibit. What is it he sees? A broken person? A crazy person? A stupid person?

I am all those things, but I'm also so much more.

It turns out, I'm also occasionally a happy person.

He sweeps his whole hand over the length of my arm and back, a soft caress that has my blood humming. He repeats the movement. "That you survived."

It's incredible how freeing it is to be authentically seen. I'd forgotten that graffiti is a form of art that often has a powerful message when it's truly understood.

Chapter Eleven

Composition: The arrangement of the individual elements within a work of art so as to form a unified whole. - *MoMA Glossary of Art Terms*

I shiver when Hendrix kisses the first of my scars.

He's not the first lover I've had who has seen them. Before Frank, I'd been guarded but less so around the men I was intimate with. I went through several boyfriends, most rebellious troublemaker sorts. Several had been quite extraordinary in bed.

But none of them—not my deceased husband, not the man who wanted to sweep me away to Brazil, not the one who broke into a pawn shop to buy me a diamond ring—not a single one of them ever pressed their lips to the raised welts scattered across my skin.

I'm stunned. And moved.

Goosebumps sprout along the path he makes. By the time he's kissed every mark on my forearm, tears are rolling down my cheeks.

He moves to my back where he lovingly kisses the cigarette burns and the barbed wire wounds and an unremembered mark he finds along my ribs.

This last one tickles, and I giggle.

Imagine me, giggling over *this*.

I'm still grinning when he gets up from the sofa and kneels in front of me. We lean into each other at the same time, our mouths meeting like old friends.

"You're beautiful," he says against my lips. "Every single inch of you."

I roll my eyes and kiss him again, a little less playfully. A little more greedily. If I am allowing myself to enjoy my body, I want to enjoy every sensation it's capable of immediately.

Hendrix doesn't seem quite as eager to speed things up as I am. "I want to kiss every place on your body you've been hurt. I want to kiss those places so many times that you remember them for that instead of anything before."

And I'm starting to remember another thing about bubbles.

He leaves my mouth to kiss up my arm again.

"When I was caught out about those—foolishly, I didn't think about the fact that the next term I'd have to wear a polo shirt for PE—I was assigned a counselor and told very strictly to stop with the self-harm." I have a reason to bring this up now. A fun reason. "Of course I pretended to comply. Really, I just started hiding where I cut."

Hendrix sits up, alert. He understands where I'm going with this. "Where are they?"

"My inner thighs." Heat rushes to my cheeks, knowing what will come next.

I'm already wet from the kissing. The rasp in his "Show me" nearly makes me come.

Making somewhat of a show of it, I lean back on my elbows and spread my legs wide. How long has it been since I've played like this with my sexual encounters? It's strange how easily it comes once I've given myself permission. I'm not even concerned about how well-lit the room is. It's a relief. It's freeing.

And that's the thing I'm remembering. That bubbles can come in streams. When you blow through the hoop. When you open a fizzy pop.

That maybe, unlike pain, these bubbles of happy weren't finite after all.

Like before, Hendrix runs his fingers tenderly across the rows of marks embedded in the soft skin at the tops of my inner thighs. There are more here. I'd discovered the delicate nature of this area made for a particularly painful cut. Since pain was what I was after, I'd done a lot of damage.

He studies each one carefully, as though trying to gather the story of each individual slice. "They're old," he remarks. "Do you still do this?"

It seems like I fight not to every day of my life. Like any addict, the more stressed I am, the harder the battle to not give in. But the help I got as a teenager taught me better ways to cope, and for the most part I've refrained since then.

I have to remain vigilant though. There's always the chance I'll fall off the wagon. Hendrix has to understand that if he really wants to be with me. Despite the happiness I find in myself under his gaze, there will always be sad days. Weeks, even. I am tentatively allowing a new future in, but it won't banish the past. "What would you do if I still did?"

"I'd kiss those marks too." As if to prove it, he bends down to place his lips on a jagged blemish at the roundest part of my thigh. "I'd love you."

I have to take a second to breathe before I speak. "The last time happened a while before Freddie was born. During a period when Frank was especially mean. It felt somehow empowering to hurt myself as well. It was pain I could control when so much of my pain came from chaos.

"After I got pregnant, though, after Frank died..." I pause to understand what I mean before I try to voice it. "I wasn't as interested in turning my body inside out anymore. I'm still tempted. But now I have more reason to not."

"I want to be one of those reasons." This time his tongue flicks across the scar. He must smell my arousal. The damp spot at the crotch of my pants is unmissable.

He kisses there next, soft and open-mouthed, his eyes on mine, seeking permission even as he invades my most private space.

I widen my legs farther in response.

I let him in.

He kisses me again, higher up. Through the silk material, he finds the swollen bud of nerves and sucks.

I let out a gasp. "Please!"

Quickly, he helps me out of my underwear and drags me to the edge of the ottoman, propping my feet up so he can take care of me properly.

And, oh, is he proper.

He's so proper, I'm already on the verge of orgasm, and it's only the third swipe of his tongue. I'd forgotten how fantastic being adored like this can be. I'd forgotten it was pleasurable at all. Frank's habit of using cunnilingus as an apology after a bad fight had, I thought, poisoned me against the act entirely.

I'm delighted to discover I was wrong.

It's only after I've come twice that Hendrix returns his mouth to mine. He's more frenzied now, tugging at the clasp of my bra as he kisses me. When my breasts are free, he plumps one with his palm while teasing and sucking the other nipple. He touched me like this in Paris, but not with his lips. The last mouth I had at my breast was my baby, and, oh God, have I been missing out.

Can't say I'm not living my life now.

It's the best life too, being cherished by a man so completely. Even when I realize I'm stark naked, and he's still wearing every stitch of his clothes, it doesn't feel uncomfortable. Of course I'm still eager for him to join me in the nudity. I pull at his Henley as he continues to feast on my breast.

Taking the cue, he abruptly stands and rips his shirt over his head. His pants tent out at his crotch, showing off a massive erection that I am eager to see in the flesh.

But when I reach for his zipper, he shoos me away. I'm bewildered until he gathers me in his arms and carries me to the nearby bedroom. He deposits me on the bed and leaves the light on as he works off his jeans.

"How long can you stay?" he asks, his eyes never leaving my body. It's amazing how they feel like they belong there, like they've always seen every part of me.

"I have the nanny until nine in the morning. I should probably be headed home by half past eight."

He glances at his watch. "Nine hours to do everything I want to do to you? I'll do the best that I can, but it's not even going to come close to being enough time."

My thighs clench with the promise. "Then, I suppose it will just have to be a beginning."

"The beginning. I like the sound of that."

Scary as it is to think, I like the sound of it too. So many of my recent stories have been rushed, begun and finished in the same night. There's a thrill in imagining how much more intricate this one can be with time, how deep and meaningful and divine.

I can see glimpses of it even now. As he rolls the condom on his cock, I foresee a night when we do away with it altogether, a promise to partner in whatever the gamble may bring. When he slides inside of me, I envision a time when it doesn't feel so new, when the excitement is overshadowed by the profundity of our love.

I see happiness that streams, even if no individual bubble lasts.

When we're sated and exhausted and he holds me against his chest, his fingers running up and down the length of my arm, I imagine this becoming routine. Imagine that it's our bed that we fall asleep in instead of his. Imagine that the sunshine that streams in the window in the morning belongs to both of us.

It's so real, I can see it. Which is exactly how art always begins.

"How much time do we have?" The sun is rising higher and the traffic on the street has picked up.

Hendrix has to shift his arm around me to check. "A little more than an hour."

I kiss along his sternum. My lips are swollen, but my mouth can't stop wanting him.

"Should we go again?"

He's noble for offering. We've already had three rounds. I've lost track of how many times I've come. My pussy is deliciously raw, and yet, I could go again. This wanting is a very deep well. It replenishes way before it's at risk of running dry.

But even though I'm as randy as a schoolboy, there is more between us than sex. And I'm very aware that my lover's attention is currently split.

"I think I'm too exhausted," I say, which is also true. I'm already working out how I'm going to trick Fred into letting us take an afternoon nap. "Besides, I feel your eyes wandering."

Hendrix plays dumb. "My eyes aren't wandering. What are you talking about?"

I twist my neck to motion to the camera sitting on the dresser. "You can't tell me you aren't thinking about it."

"Uh…" He lets out a nervous laugh before kissing me on the head. "I wouldn't dream of taking your picture without your permission."

I blush remembering my reaction in class. Was that really only yesterday? "That was…that was silly. It was about something else and—"

"I know what it was about," he says. "And I sense everything has changed, but I wasn't about to make any presumptions."

I love this show of caution, this hint that he isn't always as sure as I believe he is. It's comforting to not be alone in the awkwardness of a new relationship.

I wouldn't mind discussing that more, but this presses harder.

I prop my head up. "You see it don't you, though? What you want to capture?" I'm not sure if I'm teacher or lover in this moment. I just know what it feels like to itch with vision.

And, also, I don't want to be that woman I was yesterday. I don't want to be someone who shoves her photo albums on a shelf. I want to be the woman he sees.

He's hesitant. "Yeah, I do."

"Will they be erotic?" I tease.

"Some of them. Definitely. Are you saying yes?"

Whoa, this yes feels harder than the one when Frank proposed. When I'd thought that marriage would make him less brutal. When I'd hoped that I could settle him down.

But Hendrix isn't Frank. And I'm not who I was when I married him. Where's the proof? Everywhere.

"I am saying yes," I say, more boldly than I thought possible. Regret threatens instantly. "For your eyes only, right?"

"For *our* eyes only."

"Then...yes. Show me your best shot."

He jumps out of the bed as fast as Fred with the promise of crumpets. He throws on a pair of jeans sans underwear (hot) and strips the bed of everything but a single sheet that he allows me to use as a modest covering.

With determination in his eyes, he picks up his camera.

I'm a clumsy model, despite knowing what a photographer wants. I'm not used to being okay with the idea of being studied. But Hendrix is patient and knows how to settle the most frightened beasts. He takes his time, directing me this way and that, posing me in forms that feel strange. Pulling away the sheet entirely. Making me laugh. Over and over until my cheeks hurt from all the smiling.

When he's satisfied, he sits on the bed next to me, and without even scrolling through the pictures he's taken, he hands the camera to me.

"No self-editing first? That's brave." If he can be brave, I can be too. *Rewards.*

It's hard to look objectively at first, to not see everything I hate about myself in the foreground of every image. My pointy chin. My too-thin lips. My scars. So many times my scars.

But something happens—maybe it's Hendrix's mouth pressed to my collarbone as he peers over my shoulder or maybe it's the way he's framed the light or maybe it's the perfect composition of skin and sheet and smile. Whatever it is, I'm suddenly outside of myself looking in. I see what he meant to capture.

He's good. These pictures are so so good. An A plus if I gave grades. Exceptional and extraordinary.

And, like a good photographer, he makes me see the art instead of the artist.

So while the work itself deserves to be credited, it's not what strikes me most. What strikes me is the story he's trying to tell. What strikes me is what he sees in the woman who's me.

The woman who was always me. Always waiting for her chance in the aperture of just the right camera.

"Well?" he asks, revealing his nervousness. "Do you see it?"

I nod. I'm honest when I say the words I never thought I'd hear myself say. "I'm beautiful."

Epilogue

Perspective: Technique used to depict volumes and spatial relationships on a flat surface, as in a painted scene that appears to extend into the distance. - *MoMA Glossary of Art Terms*

As time goes by, my albums fill. Hundreds of photographs, both real and in memory form. I have favorites, of course. Images from the day Amelia, our first daughter, is born and all the milestones that follow. A series featuring Lily who pops into the world a year later with the loudest cry I've ever heard on a newborn despite being almost an entire month early. The day the adoption papers are signed and Freddie officially adds Reid to his name. The look on my husband's face when it happens, and I know no one has ever loved that boy like the two of us, together. The moment that Hendrix finally convinces me to put on his ring and make our family official.

But the albums aren't just filled with the big events. They are stuffed full of so many smaller moments. Moments that become routine. Waking up with Hendrix at my side. Clutching a baby to my breast while chasing after a toddler. Pages upon pages of child scrawled art. Picking wildflowers in the country. Watching the sunset—from the Eiffel Tower, from the Serengeti, from the beach in Myanmar, from the balcony of the flat we buy together.

I take a lot more pictures for moments and not for craft. I can't help it. I want anyone who walks into our home to see the happiness we share framed on every surface. It might inspire something in someone else who was missing it.

Becoming steady in my new self doesn't happen overnight. It takes days added upon days. It takes tears and fights and lots of doubt, but it does happen. I can see the process as I flip through the snapshots in my head. Can see the blossoming of my character in stages. I learn eventually that the more collections of these photos I have, the less I revisit the darker images from my past. As though those albums are shoved to the back of the shelf, making way for newer, crisper memories. Making way for a life fully lived. A life that extends far ahead into a beautiful distance.

* * * *

Also from 1001 Dark Nights and Laurelin Paige, discover The Open Door, Dirty, Filthy Fix, and Falling Under You.

Author's Note

Dear Reader,

Camilla's story is one I've carried around with me for quite some time. I've known who she is and what her journey had to be, but when it came to actually writing it, I struggled with how much of what I knew about her was essential to this novella. After a lot of back and forth, I decided to trust in the character and followed where her voice led me. I was surprised by the way she wanted to tell her tale, by her noisy thoughts and the depth of her wounds. It isn't an easy story, that's for sure. It definitely was the story that I needed to write at this time. When the world feels fragile and broken and unsure, I needed to believe that fragile and broken and unsure is still beautiful. I found that reassurance in this writing, and I hope you found it in the reading.

Obviously there is more to Camilla's complex history which is only hinted at here. The circumstances that led to her being in foster care and the abuse she suffered at her husband's hands as well as the circumstances surrounding his death are important parts of her character but weren't important in the telling of this particular moment in her life. Those parts of her life are further explored from her brother Edward's point of view in the Slay series. If you haven't read those books, I invite you to discover more about the Fasbender family starting with book one, Rivalry.

As always, thank you for reading.

Laurelin Paige

Discover more about Camilla Fasbender's past in Laurelin Paige's dark and edgy *Slay series*.

"This book is mean and kinky, desperate and romantic...I was consumed." - KC Caron, Goodreads Reviewer

Edward Fasbender is a devil.

He's my father's biggest rival. He takes what he wants, and he bows to no one.

And now Edward Fasbender wants me.

I didn't expect to want him back.

Having him is not in the cards, not when a union with him would destroy my father. But that doesn't mean I can't play with him a bit.

Except, I've never played against such a ruthless opponent. Edward is cold and vicious, and my blood has never run hotter. They say you should choose the devil you know, but I've always preferred long odds.

Even if it'll get me slain.

"Oh my. I was hooked. You won't be able to put this down!" - *Aleatha Romig, NYT Bestselling Author*

Rivalry is book one in New York Times, Wall Street Journal, and USA Today bestselling author, Laurelin Paige, dark and edgy Slay series.

Sign up for the 1001 Dark Nights Newsletter
and be entered to win a Tiffany Key necklace.

There's a contest every month!

Discover 1001 Dark Nights Collection Seven

VIXEN by Rebecca Zanetti
A Dark Protectors/Rebels Novella

SLASH by Laurelin Paige
A Slay Series Novella

THE DEAD HEAT OF SUMMER by Heather Graham
A Krewe of Hunters Novella

WILD FIRE by Kristen Ashley
A Chaos Novella

MORE THAN PROTECT YOU by Shayla Black
A More Than Words Novella

LOVE SONG by Kylie Scott
A Stage Dive Novella

CHERISH ME by J. Kenner
A Stark Ever After Novella

SHINE WITH ME by Kristen Proby
A With Me in Seattle Novella

And new from Blue Box Press:

TEASE ME by J. Kenner
A Stark International Novel

FROM BLOOD AND ASH by Jennifer L. Armentrout
A Blood and Ash Novel

QUEEN MOVE by Kennedy Ryan

THE BUTTERFLY ROOM by Lucinda Riley

Discover More Laurelin Paige

The Open Door: A Found Duet Novella

I knew JC was trouble the minute I laid eyes on him.

Breaking every rule in my club. I never forget how he made me feel that night. With all the women in that room, all those bodies on display, but his eyes were only on me.

Of course I married him. Now years have passed. Kids have been born. We're still in love as always, and the sex is still fantastic...

And yet, it's also not. Like many who've been married for a while, I long for the high intensity of those days of the past.

I've heard rumors for years about the Open Door. An ultra-exclusive voyeur's paradise. A place to participate in—or watch—any kind of display you can imagine.

My husband's eyes would still be on me. And maybe other eyes too. If that's what we want.

So when an invitation to come play arrives, how could we turn it down?

* * * *

Dirty Filthy Fix: A Fixed Trilogy Novella

I like sex. Kinky sex. The kinkier the better.

Every day, it's all I think about as I serve coffee and hand out business agendas to men who have no idea I'm not the prim, proper girl they think I am.

With a day job as the secretary to one of New York's most powerful men, Hudson Pierce, I have to keep my double life quiet. As long as I do, it's not a problem.

Enter: Nathan Sinclair. Tall, dark and handsome doesn't come close to describing how hot he is. And that's with his clothes on. But after a dirty, filthy rendezvous, I accept that if we ever see each other again, he'll walk right by my desk on his way to see my boss without recognizing me.

Only, that's not what happens. Not the first time I see him after the party. Or the next time. Or the time after that. And as much as I try to stop it, my two worlds are crashing into each other, putting my job and my reputation at risk.

And all I can think about is Nathan Sinclair.

All I can think about is getting just one more dirty, filthy fix.

* * * *

Falling Under You: A Fixed Trilogy Novella

Norma Anders has always prided herself on her intelligence and determination. She climbed out of poverty, put herself through school and is now a chief financial advisor at Pierce Industries. She's certainly a woman who won't be topped. Not in business anyway.

But she's pretty sure she'd like to be topped in the bedroom.

Unfortunately most men see independence and ambition in a woman and they run. Even her dominant boss, Hudson Pierce, has turned down her advances, leaving her to fear that she will never find the lover she's longing for.

Then the most unlikely candidate steps up. Boyd, her much-too-young and oh-so-hot assistant, surprises her one night with bold suggestions and an authoritative demeanor he's never shown her in the office.

It's a bad idea…such a *deliciously bad* idea…but when Boyd takes the reins and leads her to sensual bliss she's never known, the headstrong Norma can't help but fall under his command.

Man in Charge
Book One in the Man in Charge Duet
By Laurelin Paige
Now available.

The Sebastians own this city.

Hell, they own the whole world.

All I want is one little piece of it, a corner that I can call my own.

So when my boss runs away to "find herself", I seize the opportunity and dive head first into the Sebastian's glamorous universe. It's everything I've ever wanted—fast paced and high stakes—and, even though I don't fit in, I'm excellent at faking it.

Until I come face to face with the man in charge, Scott Sebastian, the arrogant, playboy heir with the mind of a devil and the body of a god and a mouth I can't stop thinking about.

He's infuriating. He's a distraction. He's the man who wants me in his bed as much as I want to be there.

And, if I get too close, he'll be the one person who could expose me for what I really am—a fraud.

Enjoy an excerpt from Man in Charge,

I turned to find myself face-to-face with the stupid-hot player, and damn if he wasn't even hotter close-up. "You," I said, a bit scornfully because I was feeling contemptuous about the way he lit every nerve in my body on fire.

"You," he said in turn. His tone seemed to both appreciate my scorn and know full well the source of it. "I was hoping we'd meet again."

"I was hoping we wouldn't."

"Funny, I don't believe you."

He wasn't an idiot, and the truth was glaringly evident. I couldn't stop staring. My eyes were magnetically drawn to him. He was so gorgeous, it made my knees weak, and I was sitting down. His hair was lighter, I realized, than I'd figured in the dark. Brownish-red with golden hues, so perfectly messy in distribution that it had to be natural. His eyes were a killer blue. I'd always been a sucker for blue eyes. And for stupid-hot player types. It was like he'd been ordered up for me specifically, a Tessa Turani cocktail guaranteed to make me mind-numbingly drunk from just looking at him.

"Can I buy you a shot?" he asked, as if I needed alcohol when he was in my system.

Somehow I managed to pull my gaze away. "It's an open bar."

"In that case, I can afford to buy you two." He summoned the bartender who hadn't gone far, that nosy little spy. "Four shots of..." Blue Eyes looked at me. "Tequila all right?"

How had he known? "The source of many a bad decision."

"Tequila it is."

He was so smooth. Much smoother than the liquor would be, I knew from experience.

Yet, I didn't object when the bartender put the four shots in front of us, along with a shaker of salt and a bowl of limes.

Just seeing the setup made me want to take my clothes off. Or maybe it was Blue Eyes that did that. He knew how to fill a tux, and I had a feeling he looked even better with it off.

He and the bartender knew exactly where this was going. How dumb was I?

About Laurelin Paige

With millions of books sold, Laurelin Paige is the *NY Times*, *Wall Street Journal*, and *USA Today* Bestselling Author of the Fixed Trilogy. She's a sucker for a good romance and gets giddy anytime there's kissing, much to the embarrassment of her three daughters. Her husband doesn't seem to complain, however. When she isn't reading or writing sexy stories, she's probably singing, watching *Killing Eve* and *Letterkenny,* or dreaming of Michael Fassbender. She's also a proud member of Mensa International though she doesn't do anything with the organization except use it as material for her bio.

You can connect with Laurelin on Facebook at www.facebook.com/LaurelinPaige or on Instagram @thereallaurelinpaige. You can also visit her website, www.laurelinpaige.com, to sign up for e-mails about new releases.

Discover 1001 Dark Nights

Visit www.1001DarkNights.com for more information.

MIDNIGHT UNLEASHED by Lara Adrian
HALLOW BE THE HAUNT by Heather Graham
DIRTY FILTHY FIX by Laurelin Paige
THE BED MATE by Kendall Ryan
NIGHT GAMES by CD Reiss
NO RESERVATIONS by Kristen Proby
DAWN OF SURRENDER by Liliana Hart

COLLECTION FIVE
BLAZE ERUPTING by Rebecca Zanetti
ROUGH RIDE by Kristen Ashley
HAWKYN by Larissa Ione
RIDE DIRTY by Laura Kaye
ROME'S CHANCE by Joanna Wylde
THE MARRIAGE ARRANGEMENT by Jennifer Probst
SURRENDER by Elisabeth Naughton
INKED NIGHTS by Carrie Ann Ryan
ENVY by Rachel Van Dyken
PROTECTED by Lexi Blake
THE PRINCE by Jennifer L. Armentrout
PLEASE ME by J. Kenner
WOUND TIGHT by Lorelei James
STRONG by Kylie Scott
DRAGON NIGHT by Donna Grant
TEMPTING BROOKE by Kristen Proby
HAUNTED BE THE HOLIDAYS by Heather Graham
CONTROL by K. Bromberg
HUNKY HEARTBREAKER by Kendall Ryan
THE DARKEST CAPTIVE by Gena Showalter

COLLECTION SIX
DRAGON CLAIMED by Donna Grant
ASHES TO INK by Carrie Ann Ryan
ENSNARED by Elisabeth Naughton
EVERMORE by Corinne Michaels
VENGEANCE by Rebecca Zanetti
ELI'S TRIUMPH by Joanna Wylde
CIPHER by Larissa Ione

RESCUING MACIE by Susan Stoker
ENCHANTED by Lexi Blake
TAKE THE BRIDE by Carly Phillips
INDULGE ME by J. Kenner
THE KING by Jennifer L. Armentrout
QUIET MAN by Kristen Ashley
ABANDON by Rachel Van Dyken
THE OPEN DOOR by Laurelin Paige
CLOSER by Kylie Scott
SOMETHING JUST LIKE THIS by Jennifer Probst
BLOOD NIGHT by Heather Graham
TWIST OF FATE by Jill Shalvis
MORE THAN PLEASURE YOU by Shayla Black
WONDER WITH ME by Kristen Proby
THE DARKEST ASSASSIN by Gena Showalter

Discover Blue Box Press

TAME ME by J. Kenner
TEMPT ME by J. Kenner
DAMIEN by J. Kenner
TEASE ME by J. Kenner
REAPER by Larissa Ione
THE SURRENDER GATE by Christopher Rice
SERVICING THE TARGET by Cherise Sinclair

On Behalf of 1001 Dark Nights,

Liz Berry, M.J. Rose, and Jillian Stein would like to thank ~

Steve Berry
Doug Scofield
Benjamin Stein
Kim Guidroz
Social Butterfly PR
Asha Hossain
Chris Graham
Chelle Olson
Kasi Alexander
Jessica Johns
Dylan Stockton
Richard Blake
and Simon Lipskar

Made in the USA
Middletown, DE
24 August 2020

16719630R00071